Turn Around

By: Geri Hemer

Dedication

This book is dedicated to mystery and its amazing effect on raising our curiosity and the quest for finding the truth. I also dedicate this effort to my readers, young adults, who I want to intrigue, indulge, and inspire to seek more!

Acknowledgment

I want to acknowledge all the people who are involved in the conceptualization and the completion of this fine story. I want to thank family, friends, and other associates who have helped me with *Turn around* as they all have a part to play in the success of this venture.

Preface

This story is about a man and woman who live in a world that is quite similar to ours. There is one major difference though. Their world exists alongside a supernatural realm, inhabited by gods, witches, and demons. This man and woman are no ordinary humans either, but they don't know it yet. By accident they stumbled upon the fact that they have been living in the midst of a tumultuous conflict between various dueling supernatural creatures.

This story will tell you how they managed overcome this revelation and eventually find the will to live for one another. I believe that books are supposed to leave their readers surprised. They should feel like they have just had a profound experience that they could have never seen coming. I wrote this novel with that belief in mind. When you read this book, you can be confident that you will not be disappointed. You will feel that you were taken on a journey that you could have never had anywhere   else.

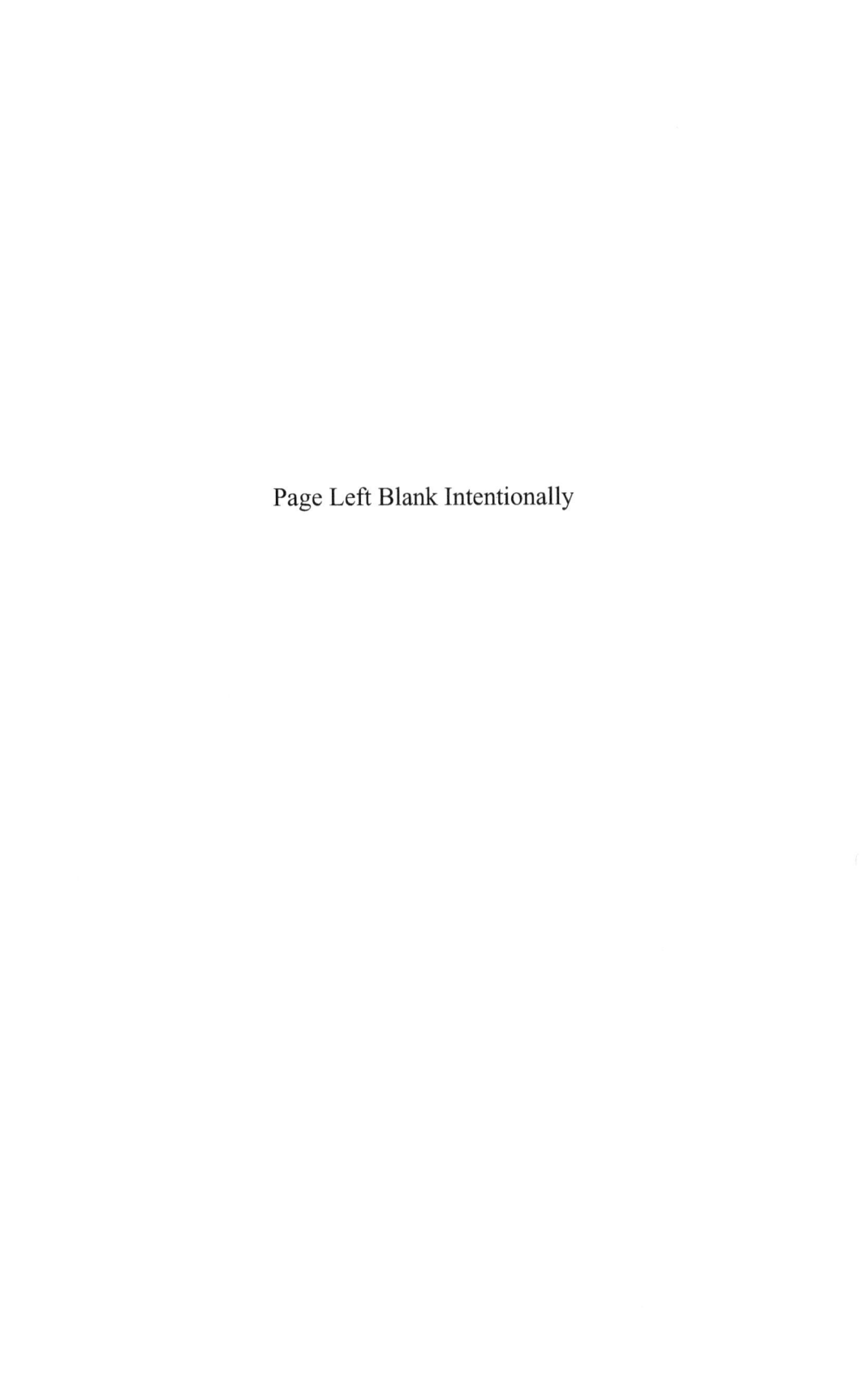
Page Left Blank Intentionally

Chapter 1
Green Bar

Another day at the bar, another day wasted. This was the life led by the apparently ordinary James Neville. He never let anyone in on his secret. It wasn't because he was ashamed or that he wished to live in isolation. Just the gravity of his situation assured him that nobody – save himself, and he wasn't even sure about that – could handle it. He went into the bar hoping today would be a bit exciting. His hopes came crashing down as soon as he stepped in from the back door and saw the same old faces busy with the same old routine.

His co-workers went about their tasks without any enthusiasm, like mindless robots. Seeing them like this, the same thought popped in his mind as always; fuck these losers and fuck my life. He knew that this gig was a waste of his time, something he didn't know he had in abundance. James didn't know his own reality. He didn't know he was as old as the first evils and the first light.

He reflected back on his life, which he couldn't quite remember. He couldn't recall anything about his childhood, his boyhood, anything. He remembered some of it, but the major parts were blurred, as if something was obstructing his memory. However, he had always been the kind of person who liked to live in the future. So he didn't really care about that.

However, he did remember something. The big hall that had his name written on it since before he had been born. He had had an entire floor entirely to himself, free to do as he wished. His parents had been weird as far as he could remember, telling him he was not theirs to keep, that he had been destined for greatness. Fuck greatness, he thought, he wouldn't want greatness if it strip teased in front of him in Megan Fox's body begging him to fuck her brains out. He thought it was partially the reason he had chosen this fucked up life as a bar manager. Still, better than being a bartender, he thought grimly.

He thought about his childhood friend, Harry, who had been at his side as long as he could remember. He couldn't quite figure out how they became friends or why they had been friends in the first place. Harry had an aura about him that James always thought was fucking stupid. If he told Harry that he had killed a hobo, he'd still find something optimistic about it. But it seemed like Harry's entire existence was to be James's companion and James couldn't be more thankful to Harry for that.

Maybe that's why he was friends with him, just because time had made him a part of James's life in such a powerful way that he couldn't get rid of him. He pushed these thoughts out of his mind for now. It made him nauseous to think about this stuff, and he tried to remember his boyhood. He couldn't quite do it though. It was all blurry. Like it happened to him in a different life. He always seemed to reflect back on the same memory… him standing in his garden, waiting to meet Harry, but he was late.

This memory was unusual to say the least; Harry was the one usually the one waiting for James. He walked around the garden and was looking at the horizon, when a lady dressed in white came up from behind and said, *"Beautiful, isn't it?"* He didn't freak out. He looked at her and somehow, he couldn't remember much of her face. All he could remember was that she was drop dead gorgeous, in a timeless sort of way. She had high cheekbones and large, stormy grey eyes. Her face was regal but cruel; like she had caused so much carnage and destruction that now she had no idea how to seem gentler.

He asked her what she wanted and then he couldn't remember what he said next, which was weird because he remembered everything perfectly up until that point. Fuck it, he pushed these thoughts out of his mind and decided to focus on the now. He looked around the kitchen area and yelled, *"HEY! Let's have some fucking drive you lazy dipshits. Look alive. You won't do it for me, at least do it for yourselves. Fucking hell."* He knew that his employees liked him so they wouldn't mind the curses, that's just how it was for them.

People couldn't get to the end of a sentence without at least cussing five times. He thought, huh, today's gonna be a good day, I'm gonna make it fucking good. Little did he know he was soon going to be plunged into the greatness that his parents had told him he was destined for. His day was about to take on a really weird turn. James went to the front of the bar and got into his usual routine, helping the bartenders set up the table. He liked doing this, it helped him focus on his actual tasks of being a manager later on in the day.

He had to do inventory, make checks out to all his employees, see that the bouncers were up so that the fuck ups, who think that the way to get a lady's attention is a bar fight, couldn't make a huge mess of the place he cared for so little. Sometimes, he wished he could accept solitude, hate companionship, and live in complete isolation. He had the money to live his life cocooned in luxury and not work a day for the rest of his life, but then he remembered that he wanted to be with someone, grow old with them, and die peacefully. He knew he could have anyone his heart wished but he could never be sure if she was with him because she loved him or because she wanted his money.

This, he remembered, was the reason he masqueraded as a pauper when in fact he actually had the money to buy the place he worked at along with any other place he wished. He wanted someone who would stick with him through thick and thin, and love him unconditionally, nonetheless. So he had recently dumped Sandy, his ex-girlfriend. Sandy had the ability to take anything and twist it to make herself the victim. She had bitched and moaned that she wanted James to work harder and provide for her so she wouldn't have to work.

She had been on his case for such a long time that he was sure, without the shadow of a doubt, that she was not the one for him. He came home from work one day, more exhausted than usual, and was preparing himself to start listening to Sandy's bullshit when something in him snapped. As soon as she started, he yelled, *"Shut the fuck up, you ungrateful bitch. If you hate your life with me so much, you have my full blessing to piss the fuck off. Actually you know what, I take that back. You don't even deserve the chance to change so get the fuck out."* He had expected her to retain some of her dignity and leave him the fuck alone, but she was adamant that she wanted to screw him to the brink of insanity. So, instead of leaving him alone, she proceeded to bitch and moan about how she could do so much better than him, which he found hard to believe. He was six foot two of pure muscle, lean and lithe as a cat. He had the cheekbones of a Greek God and a body that would put Hercules to shame.

He thought about this as he listened to Sandy's usual rant about her being better than him, and how she should have dumped him long ago. As if that wasn't enough, she started to insult his love making skills. Something about them not having had sex for the past month, which was complete bullshit because he had tried but she was the one insisted that she didn't feel well. He was glad to be rid of her and prayed a silent thanks to the universe when she finally stormed out the door. The first week was great and he had great fun chatting up the pretty girls at the bar. They just kept coming back, hoping that today would be their turn with James.

It was just too easy, James didn't even have to try. Usually saying, *"Hi,"* and offering them a free drink was all it took. He even took pride in himself that he had more game than the entire bar combined. What, with having had sex with three girls in his office upstairs, he couldn't blame himself for being smug. This didn't last though, as he soon found himself thinking of Sandy and how she would sometimes end their fights in tears, begging him to live up to his potential. She believed in him, believed that he was meant to be so much more than the manager of scrubby bar.

He couldn't tell her that he was: he somehow wanted her to prove herself to him first. She always threatened to leave him but never followed through on her threats. Maybe because she always sensed that there was something more to James than he showed or maybe because she actually loved him. He remembered how, when they did make love, she always used to do her best at making James comfortable. She would then make him a sandwich and a smoothie, chuckling to herself how he just had an intense exercise session.

He knew that as much as he wanted someone to accept him for something other than his money, what he wanted more was for someone to be with him. It was the same vicious cycle over and over again. James would meet a girl, make her feel special, loved her unconditionally and somehow she would fuck it up. Pestering him to improve in some way or the other. Eventually, James would dump her only to call her back until he met another girl; and rinse and repeat. In some way, it felt different with Sandy.

James, he chided himself, you said the same thing to yourself when it was Brenda, Joanne; and he couldn't even remember how many more. James wanted more than anything to get back with Sandy and was thinking of a plan to approach her just as the sound of the door opening snapped him out of his day-dreaming saga. As usual, it was Charlie and Roy.

When he looked at his usuals, he remembered his first thought he'd had as he walked into the bar; another day at the bar, another day wasted. He chuckled wryly at the sight of his customers. Charlie and Roy alone covered half the utilities of the bar.

James had learned that they had partnered up for a business a couple of years ago and turned a huge profit. So instead of expanding, they sold their business for a hefty sum and retired at the ripe old age of thirty. If James had a thousand guesses from looking at them about what they did, never would he have guessed that they were retired businessmen. Both of them were pudgy and barrel-chested. Favoring to wear loud Hawaiian shirt and khaki shorts, probably because those were the only things that fit them. He greeted them and they took their usual place at the bar, smack-dab down at the middle.

They had shared with James that they were hopeful that someday they would be able to chat up some girls into a threesome. How they thought they even have a chance was beyond him. He wouldn't have talked to the fucktards if they didn't cover half the running costs of the bar. He walked over to them with their usual order of two Coronas and told them to hold on for their cheeseburgers. This was what constituted for breakfast in the world of Charlie and Roy. How they were still alive and not on a ventilator was one of life's great mysteries.

Maybe millions of pounds did get them something of value. The waiter didn't even have to relay the order of two cheeseburgers to the kitchen. He just shouted, *"Charlie and Roy."* The chef knew their order by heart now; cheeseburgers, double patty, extra cheese, hold the onions and be generous with the mayo. James felt sick just thinking about it. He was talking with Charlie and Roy, and applauding them as they told him about their latest encounter with hookers.

He laughed and played along, but he wasn't really listening to them. All their stories started with the same bullshit; that they picked up hookers and fucked them till they came, and threw the money in their faces. In their stories the girls always loved them, delighted to have the chance to be their playthings for the night. They finished their story and James looked at them, wide-eyed, with, what he hoped, was jealousy but was in fact pity. He wanted them to think he was jealous of their lives so at least they would keep coming back to tell him their same bullshit stories.

They were laughing and high-fiving each other at the latest episode of this absolute travesty they liked to call life. James was just about to excuse himself so he could go to the back and be with people he hated less. As soon as he had opened his mouth, the door clicked open again and in walked the most beautiful woman James had had the fortune to look at. She was tall for a girl, almost five foot eleven. Though she didn't need to wear heels, she wore pumps that accentuated her posterior just the right amount to pass for curvy but not busty.

She walked with the easy grace of a woman who was used to turning heads wherever she went, holding her chin high just enough to let you know that she could handle anything you threw at her but not so high as to look arrogant. She had the same hairdo as Jessica Alba, but raven black, which made her look like a super model. Pair all that with her high cheekbones, large almond eyes, a pale complexion and she was James's fantasy. She had a lean and tender figure that just reinforced James's opinion that she could handle anything thrown her way.

She took her seat at the other end of the bar, placing her hands on the bar table, and her shirt dropped down just enough for James to see her cleavage. James had to grip the bar table to keep himself from falling. Just her gaze transfixed on him was enough to give James a hard on. He quickly excused himself to go into the backroom to regain composure. *"Oh God. What the fuck's happening to me?"* He had seen this woman many times, but couldn't quite place where. She looked familiar. James had often had a fleeting image of her when he was alone in bed. That had resulted in some happy times.

So why was he perspiring now and why the FUCK did he have an erection? Wasn't he just thinking about Sandy and how to win her back? So why was he looking at this beautiful stranger in his bar? Just her gaze on him had been the most exciting thing James had felt in a long time. It felt strange to feel this giddy about just a look. Get yourself together, you nitwit, James scolded himself. When he finally cooled down, he went back and out of the corner of his eye, he could see that she was still looking at him.

Maybe he hadn't cooled down as much as he had thought because as soon as he went back to Roy and Charlie, Roy asked, *"Are you sick, mate?"* Charlie added in, *"Yeah, you look like you have yellow fever."* James didn't answer them and just glanced to his right. Following his gaze, Roy and Charlie looked at the beauty and both of them muttered, *"Fucking hell!"* Roy seemed to shift to the left and James had a sneaking suspicion that Roy was going through the same sensation that James had went through just a moment ago.

He groaned, *"Why's she looking at me?"* *"Like hell, she's looking at me,"* Roy replied. Charlie didn't want to feel left out so he chimed in, *"Fuck on outta here, she's looking at me."* James looked at them both and some weird part of him wanted it to be true. He wanted nothing more than her to be one of the girls he took to the bathroom, but something held him back. He felt like he wasn't enough for her, he wanted to be the one that made her feel like she was on the top of the world. He wanted her to be his queen.

He.... he would gladly lay down his life if it meant he could be with her one minute. *"Come on boys, pull yourselves together, this ain't a strip club, you're in London's finest."* Both men jumped with a start. They couldn't believe they had been busted, and by the bar manager of all people. He hoped that would be enough for them as it was for him. James chided himself again, as he caught himself staring at her. He supposed it would do him some good to get on with his duties as the manager in one of London's 'finest.'

He groaned and set off to make sure that everything was on the up and up. Though after a while, he noticed that he was subconsciously keeping her in the corners of his eyes. He greeted some of the other regulars and they responded with concern instead of the usual bullshit greetings. He kept on replying that he's fine and wondering why he kept saying that and when had he ever been less than fine. When the tenth person asked him if he was alright, he had had enough and went back to the bar. It had been a while since James had looked at the goddess.

He felt like rewarding himself with a glance at her, and when he looked at her, he couldn't move an inch, his gaze or his body. What he saw nearly made his heart crawl up in his throat and he felt like someone had someone had tied his intestines around his lungs. He suddenly forgot how to breathe and his neck veins started bulging out. At the same place as the most beautiful girl in the world, now sat what James thought was incarnation of the Greek fates; Clotho, Lachesis and Atropos all merged into one body.

His mind couldn't think of any word to describe her other than a 'hag'. The sight of her could repel any man. The hag was wearing the same clothes as the girl but she was weirdly proportioned with fat in all the wrong places with a long crooked hook nose. Rolls of skin and belly fat protruded from under her shirt and her hair looked like it had been burned and then plastered across her scalp with tar. Where the girl had sleek and slim hands, she had what could only pass off as a weird combination of hoofs and talons; long fingernails caked with dust and grime.

The most disgusting thing about the hag was that she was looking right at James with her beady eyes and James could feel her reaching into him and beckoning him forward to just keep looking at her. It took all his will power to tear his eyes away and go straight up to his boss's room. As usual, the sick bastard was sitting on his leather-backed chair as if he was the king of the world, doing lines of coke as his girlfriend waited hungrily for her turn. He loathed both of them. 'Fucking coke-heads,' he thought disgustedly.

He especially fucking despised his boss's girlfriend, who was everything he wanted his own girlfriend not to be. If it were up to him he would bust them both, but for some weird reason he stopped himself. He knew that there would be no repercussions to his actions, whatsoever, but somehow he always managed to stop himself from beating the shit out of his boss every time the bastard so much as glanced at him. His boss looked at him and he must have sensed something was wrong because he shook his head immediately sobering up and asked him, *"What's up?"*

James made up an excuse that he wasn't feeling well and was going to take the rest of the night off. His boss didn't argue, because he knew James was an asset he couldn't afford to lose. Given the fact that almost half of the male clientele came because James was so famous among his regulars, and the female clientele came in because they had heard about James from their girlfriends. His boss looked at him with those crystalized coke-head eyes, nodded and went back to sniffing coke.

James went outside and immediately broke into a run towards his car. He wanted nothing more than to be getting as far away from the bar as soon as he could. He didn't stop or look back. He would have gone back to the bar to confirm for himself that he had imagined the whole thing up in his head. There was no fucking way that a girl that pretty could just turn into a hag like that. He was sure that he was just hallucinating but that didn't make any sense. He was not sleep deprived, nor had he engaged in any of the activities that his regulars and boss liked.

Frankly, he was scared and wanted to get the fuck away from the bar. He was sure that he would forget about the girl in the next hour or so… but fate had other plans. It was windy and comfortably cool, but James was sweating like crazy and couldn't stop his heart pounding in his chest. He ran every day at the gym so this should be nothing for him, but just the nervousness inside him made it almost impossible for him to calm down. He got in his matte black Camaro and tore off onto the road. He kept driving aimlessly, not wanting to go home but also not wanting to go anywhere in particular.

He didn't exactly pay attention to the road and floored the gas. Obviously, because it is London, some jackass kept his Chevy Impala right behind James as he weaved his way in and out of the traffic thinking that James wanted to race. He kept honking his horn and flashing the hazard light in threes. James looked into his rearview mirror and almost crashed his car into the back of a truck, but swerved at the last moment and avoided certain death. He could have sworn he saw the hag sitting in the back of his car.

It was like a mirage, her image was going in and out of focus, beckoning James to look back, to keep his gaze fixed towards her. James pulled off onto the side of the road and got out. Though he hadn't eaten anything the whole day, he barfed up all over the sidewalk and the jackass in the Chevy Impala hooted while passing him by. He knew he was imagining things but he wasn't about to check to see if the hag was still in his backseat. He locked the car and hoped to the universe that if the hag was still in there, she would die. He called his friend Harry.

"Come get me, fucking hurry," James sobbed. He knew Harry was the one person who wouldn't question him and just come as soon as possible. As always he did exactly that and just asked where he was. James incoherently explained the address to Harry and then hung up.

Chapter 2
Turn Around

James practically looked like a junkie, and he knew it. The only thing that he could think about was the old hag and how badly the mere sight of her had affected him. There was not much to be done now. He had already called Harry and told him his current address, though he had no idea how much Harry had understood. He knew that Harry should be there to pick him up any second now. He had been standing there for five minutes, but it felt like an entire lifetime. He kept thinking about how the hag had just appeared in his backseat. He had never really cared about anything much in life, and certainly didn't believe in any of the crap spewed by the religious nuts who kept raving about supernatural experiences and ghosts and shit.

He didn't believe them now either, however, it was very uncanny how he was completely sober and seeing things. James thought about the girl and his heartbeat came into control. He didn't know why thinking about her calmed her down, and even though he had just seen her for a little while, her face was completely imprinted in his memory. He felt a weird connection between him and her, as if he had known her for his entire lifetime. James had been very remarkable that way, he would always get the weirdest sense that he had seen so many things happening but he could never exactly place the memory.

It was as if somehow his mind was blocked, so he couldn't exactly think about it a lot. He was a simple man, what he did know; he accepted and what he didn't; he let go. He had perfected that over a lifetime of having the same feeling over and over again. At some point, it just got fucking old. Suddenly, everything slowed down and he felt his senses going on high alert. The Impala was way out of sight. He could see the people walking, but they were all doing the same weird walk in slow motion.

He felt someone standing right behind him, and without even thinking about it, suddenly, he grabbed the stranger by the scruff of the neck and flipped him over. He had no idea that the man was only standing there. He just felt a presence and his mind immediately assumed that it was a threat. He did all that without even thinking about it, and that was another thing that puzzled him a lot and also another reason that he was so good at his job as the bar manager. He would always end altercations before they even began. He was famous throughout the bar for never having lost a fight, ever.

No matter how many people were standing in front of him,

he would always manage to come out fine on the other end while all of them would be groaning, laying on the ground. He would then be told about the impossible feats he pulled off to take them down, and he could never figure out how he did that. He had never taken professional training, but it seemed like he had been fighting all his life. The man he had taken down just now was writhing on the ground and James looked at him. However, by that time, his mind had registered that the man was not a threat and that he had, in fact, hurt an innocent man.

He stared, flabbergasted at the man lying on the ground, cursing himself. His brain was already in overdrive and there was nothing he could have done to stop himself from judo-flipping the guy over on his back. James, bending down to pick up the guy, hoped that the man would not fight back. *"I'm sorry!"* James shouted as the man scampered off, with a certainty that he was going insane. The hag was going to get him, he had managed to put off thinking about her for a while by thinking about the girl instead. But now that this had happened, he went back into panic mode.

He had no idea how he was going to protect himself. He wasn't even sure if there was protection against whatever the fuck that bitch was. He just hoped that Harry would be able to make sense of this. *"Where the fuck is Harry!"* were the words on James's mind. He could not think why Harry was taking so long. Did he not hear the emergency in his voice? He took out his cell phone and checked the time. It had just been eight minutes since he had called him. He thought, *"How fucked am I?"* His mind was just starting to cope with the ridiculous behavior that he was exhibiting.

And simultaneously, as if something surrounding him, he picked up on his uneasiness. The mirage of the hag shimmered in front of him and he was about to collapse back into the state of mind that he was trying to escape from, even deeper than before. He had learned a lot about the power of mind over the body and knew that panic was just an abyss with no escape if not handled correctly. He used to think that people were fucking losers for not being able to control their mind, however now that this was happening to him, he found it very hard to get his feet back under him. He hoped nothing else would go wrong, so he sat down on the ground and just tried to shut his mind down. He tried to focus on menial tasks so that he could distract his mind from thinking about the hag, until Harry came. Unfortunately, he was having a lot of trouble focusing on anything except the hag right now because he could still see it standing over there, with the soul-sucking eyes peering right into his soul. Luckily, just at that moment, Harry's car screeched in front of him and broke the mirage that had appeared in front of him.

James winced. As Harry's car destroyed the mirage, James felt white-hot pang of pain in his mind that went away as soon as it came. Harry got out of the car and ran to James's side. Harry's arrival was just in time. James was almost at his wits end and had almost collapsed. The panic and exhaustion were too much for his brain to handle. The previous thoughts about not wanting to go home went right out the window as soon as he saw Harry. Maybe it was just the fact that James was so scared already, that it was becoming impossible to get out of the panic.

Now, all he wanted to do was get to his home, where he would, hopefully, be safe from the hag and the unnatural control she had over him. Seeing Harry, his rational mind started churning the motors again, and he figured out that the hag was just a figment of his imagination. Since it was a figment of his imagination it had taken control of his mind and he knew that he would have to calm down before he was free of the hag.

Harry came onto his side and steadied him. *"What happened?"* he asked calmly. This was the best thing about Harry. He was able to stay calm even in the worst situations, and was able to make the hardest obstacles that life threw at him bearable. He was there for James, even when James was not there for himself. He had saved him so many times from all sorts of situations that could easily have been avoided, had James had a bit more self-control. He was usually all over the place, and maybe, hopefully, James thought, this was just one of those times.

"I was at the bar...this woman, no, girl. This girl came...sat down and turned into Satan," James gasped and looked to Harry for acknowledgment. In James's mind, he had succinctly described his entire situation in a sentence. Harry was looking at him blankly. However, James could tell that Harry's eyes were filled to the brim with concern. That was usually the case whenever something even slightly out of the ordinary happened to James. When James had calmed down, after whatever happened he thought about why Harry was always so concerned about him.

Even though Harry was James's best friend, he seemed way more concerned about him than a best friend would be. Almost as if he had been waiting for that particular thing to happen. James always brushed the thought away from his mind though, thinking that maybe that was just the way Harry was. The situation this time was very different than usual, he knew what he had seen, and since he was completely sober without even a single drop of alcohol or drugs in him he was afraid that this was some next level shit he was dealing with.

In his state of mind, however, James thought that Harry

might not be taking him seriously, and shouted another explanation at him, *"I'm telling the truth, Harry. I swear she was sitting there all pretty one second then I looked at her again and she was Satan, like a hag. She is here, Harry. I saw her. Take me home!"* James shouted. Harry did not care who was looking at him, nor did he care what they were thinking of him. *"Calm down. I'm taking you home. Don't sweat it,"* Harry said soothingly.

James was damn sure that he was safe in Harry's hands, though he was not sure how much of what he had said Harry actually believed in. *'I am not insane'*, James had to keep reminding himself. Mostly because he was sure that the things that had happened to him didn't usually happen to normal people. He had seen the old hag in the place of the girl that was sitting at the bar, and he had seen the old hag in the back of his car. That much was for damn sure. He still could not figure out how or why he had felt the white-hot pang of pain in his mind, or why he had heard her say something, but he was sure that he had not imagined it.

The pain had gone almost as soon as he had he felt it, and her voice felt more like he had talked to himself. *"Jesus James, calm down. You are safe. Now start from the beginning, what happened?"* Harry asked in a calming voice, as he was concerned about his oldest friend. He was sure that James was not taking drugs, it was one line that he would never cross. Why he was acting like this was beyond Harry, and it seemed to be beyond James as well. James had not said a single coherent sentence since he had gotten into Harry's car. Instead he stared at space and whispered gibberish. However, the sound of Harry's voice managed to tear through the cloud of fright and haze that surrounded James' mind. *"I don't know how to explain this, Harry. She just changed."* James said, looking at Harry, hoping that he would understand this simple yet loaded statement. Before this. Every time something even remotely weird happened, James had been able to bring himself to talk about it. But, this time he could not even explain himself because he mentally could not make sense of the situation. He felt that his mind had completely turned into mush. *"So let me get this straight. There was this woman, or girl, that came into the bar. Then, after some time, you looked at her and she was Satan?"* Harry said, somehow keeping his composure during all of this.

He was not one to laugh at his friend's problems, but the idea was ludicrous. Even though Harry was trying to make light of the situation he knew that deep down, his friend was very concerned for him. *"Harry, she turned into this old crooked woman. She was so ugly, like the Three Fates. Remember? We read that book?"* James said, laboring to keep his composure. He was still panicked, yet able to think straight

24

now. Remembering what he had said to Harry, he felt embarrassed and lost any confidence he had built. So he decided to rephrase himself as best as he could. *"Listen, I'll tell you from the beginning. I was talking to Charlie and Roy. Then this girl came in. Bro, she was Aphrodite's incarnation. Like a solid 10 outta' 10. I looked over once and then went to the regulars, to talk to them.*

When I came back and looked over again, in her seat...like exactly where she was sitting, there was this other old hag – don't you dare fucking laugh, you asshole," James said as the barest hint of a smile broke through Harry's face. *"Sorry man, but honestly... Hag?"* Harry chuckled.

"Will you just listen, please? She was looking right at me and I felt so weird and nauseated and I swear, I can't describe the feeling. I couldn't stand there, so I came outside and then I got in the car. I can't remember exactly what had happened then, but I do remember that I saw her face in the rearview mirror and almost crashed the car. I stopped the car and got out and, I swear, I hadn't eaten anything all day and somehow I ended up barfing," James said, keeping it as simple as possible.

He was not about to give Harry any more opportunities to giggle at him. Though judging by the look on Harry's face, he wasn't in the mood for giggling anymore. James had noticed the subtle change in Harry's expression as he talked, however he was way too preoccupied for anything to register in his mind. He was already feeling so inadequate that he could not get the image of the girl out of his mind. Thinking of her had made him horny. He was with Harry, so he pushed these thoughts out of his mind.

Harry looked at James, feeling a rush of concern for his best friend. Even though he had an inkling of where this was headed, he knew better than to just tell his best friend everything. His friend's wellbeing and mental stability was above everything, and right now he needed somebody to talk to about what had happened. Harry knew the kind of person James was. He was sure that he would have appreciated an explanation, however, Harry knew better than to give one to James right now.

It was kind of like being a parent, you just had to watch your child fuck up every once in a while so that they can find their own way. Although in James's case this was the story of his life, he was bound in the same cycle, doomed to repeat it for all of his life. Harry knew quite a lot about James, more than he did himself, and that's why he understood what was better for James, and for the rest of the world. *"Look, we'll talk about this, okay? Let's go up to your apartment so you can freshen up,"* Harry said.

It was not funny anymore, and the smiles and chuckles were disappearing from his face. He was all serious now. There was not a trace of humor in his eyes or face now. It was replaced with determination and anger. It had been the same cycle ever since he had known James, which was his entire life. Even though James' mind was preoccupied with all that had been happening, he still noted the anger in James's eyes. This confused him, however, that could wait; he had other things to worry about. He could not think about anyone else right now. He had to focus on making sense of the entire situation, or else he would go insane.

"Listen, I'll be okay. I'm probably overreacting. I'll call you in a while, why don't you go on?" James said, half-heartedly. He did not want his best friend to leave him at a time like this. But he also did not want to appear weak. For all that had happened to James in his life, he had never once considered himself to be weak, nor had he acted like one. He knew that the world was fucking cruel, and if he showed any sign of weakness, it would trample him to his grave. Being strong had become sort of second nature to James. Right now, however, he was pretty sure that he was far, too far, away from being

'okay.' Harry saw past the bullshit and replied the only a best friend could.

"Fuck on upstairs, will ya? I'm coming back with some food," Harry replied and winked. He was sure that his friend needed him right now and no amount of bitching and moaning, on James part, would drive him away. He had been a part of James's life ever since he was born, and he knew everything about James, so he knew that James would try to push him away as well. He also knew that he could never let James do that. *"Dude..."* James said, considering blowing Harry off, but after what had happened, he didn't really want to be alone. *"Fine, I'll be waiting upstairs."* James caved in gladly. He was thankful that Harry understood his situation. Now that he thought about it, he was actually quite hungry, and that made him all the more thankful to Harry for going to get him some food. James started walking into the building and up to his apartment. Each step he took, in the lobby, towards the elevator, was harder than the step he took before. He somehow finally got to the elevator and pushed the button, getting in and going up to his penthouse.

Now that he was alone with his thoughts, there was a nagging sensation in his pants. He had never been this way before, he had been so desperate for a girl, his girl, his entire life. As a very good looking bar manager, he had snagged his fair share of girls, each one hotter than the one before. It was so easy for him that he actually challenged himself to make it as hard as possible to pick up girls, coming up with wild stories to get their attention.

He once convinced a girl at the bar was actually a front for MI6, and he was a secret agent. So he was good with women, but that girl at the bar had turned his world upside down.The thoughts of her kept intruding and made him want to get as quickly as he could to his apartment so that he could be alone... preferably with a bottle of Vaseline and Kleenex. He was not thinking about any of the girls he had been with in the bar, nor the ones whom he had taken back into his apartment. He was not even thinking of his ex-girlfriend. He just wanted to be in his own company, and he felt that urge strongly. So strongly, in fact, that there was almost a moment when his eyes clouded and he felt like collapsing on the floor. He was still in the elevator and he had to get a grip on himself. His fucking heart was actually pumping so much blood over to his dick that his vision was clouding. After exercising what seemed like an enormous amount of restraint on his part, James pushed the thoughts of that temptress from the bar from his mind and went to his apartment. There, he laid down on his bed and turned on some music. He searched for death metal music and turned it to the loudest and put on his headset. He was willing to try just about anything to divert his attention from the girl in the bar, but he remained unsuccessful.

The only thing that he succeeded in doing was remind himself of her, and even the incessant screaming wasn't able to push her out of his mind. He had no idea why the fuck he was listening to death metal, he hated the stuff. It's just that he thought that that would make diverting his attention from her a bit easier. Unfortunately, that wasn't the case. The vision of her kept crawling back into his mind. When he couldn't stand it any longer, he finally gave in and tried to recall everything he remembered about her. She was absolutely perfect. Tall, graceful, with a sleek and petite figure.

Everything about her made James go crazy. Most of the girls in the bar would either dress up like sluts or like slobs. It was rare to find a girl who was classy, and that's what this girl was. She had been wearing simple jeans, and a white silk shirt that accentuated her butt in the most amazing way possible. On top of that she was also wearing knee length boots, James's favorite and a leather jacket. Everything about her assured James that she was the one for him. The way she walked, not too arrogantly, nor too meekly, sent the message that she would not appreciate any jackass approaching her and ruining her mood. Her eyes seemed so deep, as if they could hold the entire universe inside of them. Suddenly James felt someone jerking him up. *"Get the fuck up, will you? What the fuck are you listening to?"* Harry shouted as he pulled James' headset off his head and the death metal reached his ears. James had been lying with his eyes closed, completely oblivious to Harry's presence. Harry had used his key to enter the apartment, and had seen him lying on the bed with headsets on. James was so startled that he accidentally kicked Harry in the chest.

"Watch out, you halfwit. It's me, Harry," he yelled. He was startled too that James had attacked him. James stopped just in time as he was about to kick him again. He backed off and started laughing. *'Maybe that was what I needed to cheer up.'* James thought *"Yeah, very funny. Fuck off,"* Harry replied angrily. *"I brought you food. Cheeseburgers and milkshake. You need to lay off the beer and whiskey."* James looked at Harry and smiled, getting up from his bed. He saw the McDonald shopper lying on the dining table and quickly washed up before gorging on it. Even though he had just barfed up and was nauseous, the food felt great and there was pin drop silence until he finished eating. Then, he sat silently with Harry. Both of them were unsure of how to breach the subject of what had happened to James at the bar. Finally, James broke the silence.

"Listen, I wasn't lying about it. There was some weird shit

going on today at the bar. I told you what I saw. I wasn't shitting you and you know I ain't on drugs or any of that shit." James kept saying that. Both of them knew that he hated the shit, and that he would never even go near it, but that seemed like the only explanation that would make sense. If James looked at it logically, what he had experienced was a hallucination, which could only be induced by drugs. *"I didn't even have anything to drink, in case you were thinking somebody slipped me something,"* James said as logically as he could.

"James, I never said I didn't believe you. There are a lot of things that are possible in this world. I just want to make sure you are okay. You are fine, right?" Harry asked. *"I am not sure yet. You wouldn't be fine either if something like that happened to you. There was literally no explanation for what had happened,"* James replied. Harry had a knack for never panicking. No matter how bad things got, he would always retain composure. James had always felt that he was the same way, however he could never quite manage to give the same cool and calm reaction to everything as Harry did.

He would try to be calm, or get back to being calm as quickly as he could, but he would somehow fail. It was as if his mind was not ready to be calm. He knew he had it in him, but something was just... blocking it. *"Let me ask you this – is there anything you can do about it right now?"* Harry asked, and without waiting for an answer went on to say, *"No, right? Then push it from your mind. Deal with it when the time comes, if you have to,"* Harry said. James felt a little uncomfortable at the way Harry phrased his words, but he could not be bothered with that right now. Harry always had a way of saying things that were perfectly diplomatic. He would just make a statement, neither confirming nor denying anything, nor taking any sides. That always pissed James off to no end, however right now he had things to do other than fight with James. The thought of that girl had again brought about him an uncontrollable urge to be alone. *"I understand, bro. I'll be fine. I am a bit tired. I'm going to sleep, okay?"* James said. This time he meant it. He wanted to be left alone to deal with this. *"Sure, man. I'll call you tomorrow."* Harry said before getting up to leave. With that, James was now all alone.

Chapter 3
The Carnival

Lucille Idona was feeling foolish after having come to this carnival with her friends, Betty and Jean. She knew all about the kind of tricks they pulled here and was well aware on how to deal with scam artists. She was an educated woman and rather pretty as well. She was confident and knew that she was in fact, a deadly combination of beauty and brains. She knew how to use her strengths to her advantage.

And one thing she was certain about; she would never use either of these resources to stoop to the level of the scammers that fooled anyone who ventured into their tents. Lucille had always hated them with a passion. She knew that some people actually believed in this crap and went to fortune-tellers for help in actual, real world problems. They would never believe that they were just being ripped off by a person who could just act really well, and be melodramatic when the situation called for it.

Ever since she was little she had been made to believe that there was another dimension that existed within our own world and that we should never come in contact with it. Normal people had no idea that this dimension even existed and had no idea that messing with could be dangerous they could die! She denied that fact with all her heart, however a small part of her wanted to believe that it was true. Not because she was crazy like those jackass emotional fools, but because she wanted to believe that her lineage did not consist of druggies and lunatics. She had been led to believe that a supernatural element, something older than time itself, and just too complex for the human mind to comprehend, existed right alongside us. It was something normal people could neither feel, nor see. And those who could, were often met with blank stares and declared chemically unstable by the people around them.

There were just some things that the human mind did not want to see nor understand, and that was this supernatural world, that existed, but was simultaneously hidden. At least that is what she had been told. She had let that part of her life go a long time ago but it was very hard to convince yourself that your mother, your aunt, your grandmother were insane. Lucille did not even know who the fuck her father was, nor was she inclined in any way to track him down. As far as she was concerned he was dead to her, just like her mother was. At least her mother had stuck around long enough to make sure that Lucille could survive by herself.

And when she did leave, Lucille was placed in her aunt's care. She knew that everything the fortune-tellers claimed to believe or do was real as well, however the way they did it made it insanely clear that they were nothing like the people who actually possessed these skills, like Lucille's grandmother did. It was quite frankly an insult, and it was one that would never hold. She knew all this because she had descended from the line of the 'apparently' great Ida Idona, who was revered in the northern areas, around the parts where Landsend Castle was located, according to Lucille's mother. Lucille never bothered to find out if anything her mother had told her when she was young, was the truth. She just wanted to distance herself as much as she could from that phase of her life and for a long time she had been quite successful at doing just that. She had no intention of being sucking into it again but her history was a part of her. She had tried her very best to forget everything, she went through in her childhood, and move on with her life.

However every so often she was reminded that she was not the same as everyone else in the world. At least not anyone that she knew. She had come across no other descendants of Ida Idona, nor any other seer with whom she could talk to about her childhood. Lucille laughed at the thought. She had been going through this for a long time. She had tried a lot to stop thinking about the things that happened when she was young. But she could never quite manage that. However, she did know that she needed therapy to overcome this, and find some mental peace. Since she had never found anyone to talk to about this kind of stuff she had resorted to talking to herself.

She had a weird ability, she would disassociate from herself and then talk to herself calmly about the situation at hand. Just like now; she was thinking about her past and she was telling herself that she should stop doing it. However before she knew it, she was thinking about it again. This was the only aspect of her life she could never make up her mind about. She was always conflicted about this and the only time she was at ease was when she was treating another person.

Lucille's mother had told her of the goings on in Landsend Castle, telling her the story of the witch, Lumis Ash. Whenever Lucille was having a hard time with anything in her life, her mother would tell her this story. She remembered clear as yesterday when she had first heard it; when she was barely two and a bully was picking on her. She went to her mom and said, *"Mom, Big Bertha is a mean girl. She pulled my hair today and pushed me to the ground." "I see, Lucille,"* her mother said lovingly. She wasn't the typical mother. But one would sort of expect that when you have led your life being the daughter of one of the greatest seer's in the entire world.

She had lost the ability to look at the smaller things and was always focused on the bigger picture. She knew that she had to make her daughter strong for what was to come. Being the daughter of a seer she always knew that her daughter was going to face a lot of hardships in life and she could not just let her be weak, ever. And so, she began *"Come here sweetie, let me tell you a story."*

Her mother picked her up and made her sit on her lap and began, *"Long before you were born there was a woman who lived in the north. She was very beautiful and everywhere she went, she would spread joy and happiness. Her name was Ida. She was wise and she was humble. She could never bear anyone's pain and always knew that she had to help them, no matter what the consequences. So you can guess that she was always loved and respected wherever she went."*

She remembered that her mom got misty eyed and look at her feet. She continued, *"She never could see anyone suffering in a hardship, always choosing to take that person's place or at least share in their pain. So naturally, she was pretty famous in that town. But you know what they say, right? For every Yin there is Yang. And so was the case here. Where Ida lived, there also lived another woman, Lumis... Lumis Ash."*

"She lived alone in a castle, away from the main town. Some say that she was driven there and some say that she isolated herself there due to her hideousness. I don't know what really happened. Anyway, Lumis was always jealous of Ida. She was jealous of her beauty, her smarts and her fortune telling abilities."

Her mom would stop at this point, to smile at the look of wonderment that Lucille had on her face.

"Yes, that is right. Ida was a seer. Do you want to know what her last name was?" She asked her child.

"No, mom," she said

"Her last name was Idona, just like yours and mine." Her mother laughed, *"So think about this. You come from from the greatest, you are of the greatest. So do you think that one child being mean to you is something that you can't handle? You are strong. You are the one who is going to be great."*

Her mom would always end the story with this declaration. Somehow, this was the very few memories she had of her mom before she died. More accurately, when she disappeared. Lucille's mother had went away when she was just two years old. As far as Lucille could remember, it was the very night she had told her that story. It was almost as if her entire life was leading up to this point, where she would tell this story to her daughter and then leave forever. Her disappearance was shrouded in mystery. She just up and disappeared, leaving Lucille all alone.

This was also one of the reasons she was inclined to believe that there was something otherworldly going on in this world; something that not everybody quite knew about. Something was not quite right with the way her mother had disappeared. It had happened so long now that there was no hope of ever getting her back. Lucille just accepted the inevitability that her mother was dead. She had internally accepted this as a fact a long time ago, but there were some things about her disappearance that still bothered her. For example, when she got older, she was told that her mother was taken in the middle of the night.

One moment she was there and the next, she just disappeared. Since she was a child, her mother's disappearance was something spoken about in hushed whispers around her. But she heard it all. It was completely absurd, the way that people claimed that her soul was taken in the middle of the night by the devil. It was said that her mother had breached some sort of agreement with the devil or angered a powerful witch who had come after her for vengeance. Lucille did not believe in any of this fairy tale bullshit.

She was a grown woman and had her own beliefs. She was not about them let that go just because others believed some stupid local folklore. She also remembered the most absurd encounter that had taken place in her life. It was her sixteenth birthday and she had just come home. Her aunt, whom she lived with, sat her down as soon as she got home from school. It seemed like it was something important. *"Lucille, dear. Please come here and sit with me,"* she said, dread filling her eyes. This was peculiar for her, as she was typically a very happy woman.

"Are you okay, auntie? You look troubled," Lucille asked, worried that she was about to get some bad news. Whatever it was, she was prayed that it wouldn't have much of an effect on her birthday celebrations. She was already so stressed about her exams and school that she just needed this chance to party. *"I need to tell you something. It's about your mother. She told me to tell you this, long before you were born. She told me that if she had a daughter, that I should tell her to never have her palm read."*

She looked deadpan serious about this. Lucille kept waiting for the punchline, though it never came. Was this her idea of a joke? She wondered if she had called her in here only to tell her that before she was born, her mother asked her to tell her never to have her palm read. *"Sweetie, I know it sounds absurd, but please just listen to me. Do you remember that time your mother told you about your great grandmother, Ida Idona?"* she asked Lucille, still completely serious about this conversation.

"Yes. What are you going on about?" she asked, through gritted teeth. It was one thing to play a prank on her, but completely another to drag her mother into this. She should have known how sensitive Lucille could be when her mother

was brought up in conversation. *"Do you remember the witch that she told you about? Her name?"* she asked. *"I don't remember the whole thing. Just the overview. Something about me coming down from a line of powerful women, so that nothing could harm me, that I was strong and that I was destined to be a great woman,"* Lucille whispered, barely able to keep it together because she was so sensitive about her mother.

"Your great grandmother was a seer. She told it to our mother, your grandmother, that Lumis Ash, the witch who lived in Landsend Castle, had cursed our entire family. The first girl to be born in the next three generation, who had her palm read, would be cursed for life. I don't know what curse that might be. All I know is that you should never have your palm read. Are we clear?" she said seriously, her voice had changed. She meant every word of what she'd just said.

Lucille had just seen her like this once, before when she had made her promise that she would never smoke again. She wanted this conversation to be over with, as soon as possible. So she just said, *"Sure, aunt. Don't worry."* Lucille did not know what that was about, but she did know one thing for sure. She was not going to fall for this bullshit. She did not care about anything. However, something deep down inside of her, tugged at her soul, assuring her that these myths were based on facts and this Lumis Ash must have been someone real nasty. But out of sheer stubbornness, she refused to accept what that voice told her, she was sure that it couldn't be anything more than nonsensical myths. She was determined to live a normal life. She had grown up just like that, refusing to even think about her mother's disappearance, or that mysterious woman, Lumis Ash. She had grown up to go to university and then graduate at the top of her class; eventually becoming a therapist.

She did her best to help people come out of their trauma, comforting them as they worked through it, or in severe cases, just forgot it. However, there was another reason she had become a therapist. She wanted to learn how trauma affects the human mind. She had been through shit herself, and since there was no therapist available to counsel her through the bullshit spewed by her mother and her aunt about her great grandmother, she decided that she would learn everything how to deal with her issues herself.

She had become her own therapist, using her ability to completely disassociate herself from her own being. She often tried to think rationally about the night her mother had told her that story, the same night when she died and left her all alone. Ever since she became a licensed therapist, she had also been using her knowledge to cater to other people going through shit like herself. She loved helping people, however, she knew that unless and until she was able to completely work through everything that had happened in her childhood, she would never be able to completely heal and fix anyone else.

As she looked around her, she knew that she was surrounded by some of the best scam artists in the world. Even though she paid no heed to her aunt's warning, she still did not fancy going to any of the fortune tellers that were in the carnival. Lucille was a woman with impeccable principles and morals. She would never have compromised on them.

She had been that way ever since she could remember; going through so much pain during childhood tends to have that effect on a person. Lucille had learned that the characteristics that people exhibit as adults, are somehow related to their childhood experiences. All their experiences correlate to their actions in some way or the other, which explained her personality.

"Oooohhh! Look, there is one of those fortune tellers, wanna go in and see who's gonna be the first one of us to get laid?" Betty laughed.

She was always the one to suggest the craziest things, in fact it had been her idea to come to the carnival in the first place. Three grown women, all of them with serious careers, coming to a place where horny teenagers come to make out and find secluded spots to bone. Lucille laughed, because just then she saw two kids doing the walk of shame coming out from behind a tent. She looked at them longingly.

She had never had the chance to do that because she could never give herself up that easily and when she did, she regretted it because the guy turned out to be a douche. However, she still believed that there was the perfect guy for her out there. It was hardwired into her brain. She held firmly to the belief that there is some guy who is meant to be hers completely and fully. *"Let me save you your twenty bucks right here, Betty. It's gonna be me,"* Jean smirked. *"Yea, I'm not too sure about that. It could be this nun,"* Betty said, pointing to Lucille, who had been out of it since they came here. Her instinct kept telling her that something was about to go wrong. It was so frustrating, being at a place she would have loved otherwise, and her gut kept on bothering her. She was not too fond of the idea of going to the fortune teller.

"I'm in! Lucille, come on," Jean said, locking arms with Lucille and dragging her forward. *"Guys, please I don't want to,"* Lucille managed to say, just before they entered the tent of Ms. Abisai. As soon as she entered, the smell hit her... and

then she heard the faintest laughter; more like a cackle. *"Did you hear that?"* Lucille asked. She knew that she had not imagined that. However neither Betty nor Jean had given any indication that they had heard the cackle.

She knew that she was just being paranoid, having thought of her mother and grandmother just before entering the tent, but she could not shake the feeling that the cackle was almost as if someone was satisfied that she had come here. She had not given her aunt or mother the slightest thought for a long time. They were in the past, and as far as she was concerned they had nothing to do with her now. *"Heard what?"* Betty asked, looking amused. Lucille knew that she would just blow her off and make another joke, but she had to find out if she had actually heard the cackle.

"That laughter?" Lucille asked, dead serious. She was not in the mood for jokes right now and actually wanted to find out if she had actually heard the laughter. *"Haha, sweetie…"* Jean said, looking a bit concerned, *"you're just trying to scare us now."* Lucille looked at them both and knew that they were not joking, so she decided to drop it. *"Well that is what you fucking get for dragging me into this shit hole,"* she said while laughing. She had no intention of being the subject of Betty or Jean's scrutiny right now. All she wanted really was to get out of there as soon as possible, but her friends were stubborn as

all hell. They would not let her leave until and unless they had their palms read by the fraud, Ms. Abisai. She had never told anyone about her childhood and had no intention of telling them right now so she just decided to drop it.

"Kill yourself, please?" Jean said, exasperated. Lucille finally put her finger on the smell; it was like someone had sex and used rotten fish to lubricate themselves. She tried to turn around and walk out but just then the most disgusting looking woman walked out from behind a curtain. *"Welcome! Ms. Abisai was forewarned about your arrival. You!"* she pointed towards Lucille. *"You are afraid of me,"* she stated, her voice raspy and her appearance like a hobo. Lucille thought, 'who the fuck does this woman think she is, pointing at me like that.' Even the tent was weirdly furnished. Nothing matched and it looked like everything was taken off of the street. The curtains in the tent were purple and the cushions on which they were invited to sit were mustard color. They were so dirty they might as well have been red. She cursed her friends for dragging her in here.

"I am afraid of you? I suppose, yes. Since you smell like the rotten carcass of a sewer rat. I would much rather drag my bare ass through broken glass than be here." Lucille shot back. Now she knew that that was way out of line, but she was very much on edge now. She couldn't shake the feeling that

47

something was about to go so wrong that it would affect her entire life. Both Betty and Jean hid their faces in their hands to stifle their laughs. *"I would hold my tongue if I were you, girl,"* the gypsy snarled. *"If you could see what I see, then you'd shiver. I will tell you, it is important. But first you have to pay."*

"This oughta be fun," Jean laughed out loud, unable to hold it in, at the gypsy and Lucille, who were having a stare down. She was inclined to get things started so that they could have a good time. So she took out the twenty bucks and gave it to the gypsy. *"Sit down,"* the gypsy said, pointing to the couch. Lucille sat down but never broke eye contact with her. She was pissed at the way she talked to her. The bitch thought that she was the queen of the world, scamming naïve fuckers out of their money.

She knew very well that neither Jean nor Betty gave two shits about what this woman had to say, but this was just their idea of fun. *"Oh goodie, let's see what load of crap this hag has for us,"* Lucille said in an undertone to Jean and Betty, who had to stifle their laughs yet again. She continued frowning at the gypsy. *"So tell me, what do you wish to know?"* The gypsy asked. *"Ooooh! I know,"* Jean piped up, faking enthusiasm, while Betty hid her snickering. *"She wants to know when she'll get laid,"* she said, pointing towards

Lucille.

Lucille looked at both of them exasperated. She could not believe these morons were wasting their twenty on this. *"Give me you palm then. I will tell you who your next love interest will be,"* the gypsy said, her hand outstretched. Then, something weird happened. As soon as her hand touched her, the gypsy started shaking. She was shaking her head, like she was being strangled, but all this time she never let Lucille's hand go.

Her whole body vibrating, both Jean and Betty thought that this was all part of the performance, and that she would be back to normal in a while, to tell Lucille that her next love interest is going to be a tall, dark handsome buck, who is going to rock her world. Just as suddenly as she had started shaking, she became still. Looking up, she locked eyes with Lucille and said one sentence, after which Lucille lost consciousness. *"My name is Lumis and I have been waiting almost eighteen years for you. I thought you will never give me another chance.."*

Chapter 4
Lumis Ash

The next time Lucy opened her eyes, she was sitting in a bar. She felt alien to her own body; like she was there, but was being controlled by something else. She immediately hated that feeling. She was disgusted by it. It felt like she was being raped, not physically but mentally. She just knew that she was seeing, except that she could not do anything. It looked like she was in a bar, somewhere. She tried to understand what was going on.

She remembered the last thing that had happened and she felt the chill spreading to her bones. She didn't really want to go to the fortune teller but it had nothing to do with the warning that her aunt had given her when she was young. It was just because she didn't want to compromise on her morals by aiding the life of a fraudster but this had turned out to be something completely different and entirely unnerving.

For a moment she thought that she was having a lucid dream. But this felt way too real to be a dream. She had no idea how she ended up in that situation, one moment she was sitting in a tent and the next she was here in a bar, merely a spectator to her own actions. She tried with all her might to gain control of her own body but she could not even come close to moving a finger. She had never felt this way in all her life.

She did not want to believe the fact that the fortune teller had said that her name was Lumis and she had complete blacked out and ended up here, with no control over her body. She had no other choice but to think about what her aunt had said. Plus the weird things that were going on right now, right after she had done exactly what she had been told not to do. It was all too much. She cursed herself. She should have resisted her friend's insistence for getting the fortune teller to read her hand.

Now, she had done something so stupid that it was incomprehensible. She had gone against the advice of her grandmother and now paying the price for it. She did not believe a thing she had found out about her grandmother or her mother. All of that was just plain stupid and she was a grown and educated woman who couldn't possibly fall for that ancient load of bull. She had spent the better part of her life trying to get away from her childhood. Having their mother disappear on them and not even knowing how was disorienting as it is.

That would have been too much to process for anyone in the world. And the best fucking part, she had then been told never to get her palm read because of some age old fucked up stupid rivalry. She knew that she should have been very afraid that she was in whatever this situation was, but right now she was just fucking pissed. This was perhaps the most absurd situation that she had ever been in. She thought about how this situation would end, and she knew that if it ended with her death she would probably die from trying to process the lunacy of everything she had been exposed to in life, instead of any physical injury. She handled the absurdity of her life the only way she knew how. She suppressed it to the point that it hardened into a lump within her. Her entire life had been affected by her mother's disappearance. She had made stupid choices so many times, but she had always come out fine on the other end.

This time around, however, she had made the dumbest mistake of her life. Slowly the reality of the situation started to settle in. She tried to think about it; she had been at the fortune teller who had told her out of the blue that she was Lumis and now she had no control over her body. She was fairly certain that she was in some sort of limbo. She was not really sure how she would get out of it, but she knew that she had to try.

She cursed herself again for the mess she had gotten herself into. She had done the one thing that she was told expressly not to do. She knew that she could not count on her stupid friends to come and bail her out. They were probably too stupid to even notice that something weird had happened. Fuck those bitches! Why had she even allowed them to drag her to the fortune teller? It was their fault that she was now in this fucked up place.

She then started paying more attention to her current circumstances, realizing that her entire body felt different. It felt like it was hot. She hadn't noticed this before, but now it was apparent. It was like she was slowly simmering in a stew and the temperature was getting hotter and hotter. She tried to control it, and tried to get up to move outside. But all to no avail. She had no control and no matter how much she fought, it was like she was losing more and more control with each passing moment. She was completely immobilized and couldn't feel the source of this heatwave. She did not feel like she had a body. It was like she was thinned out and was like the particles in air and each particle was being burned separately.

She was already being stretched out and now she felt pain. Like needles were being pushed through her skin. It was a testament to her hard headedness that even through the pain she was still trying to think clearly about what she could do to get out of that situation. She tried to recall anything from her childhood that would help her in this situation, and she remembered that her mother had once said to her, *"You are strong. Nobody can control you. Remember that. It is of utmost importance. Use the strength you have inside you and overcome the problems you are facing."*

She had no idea where she got this memory from. She thought that she might be imagining it up because it hadn't been there before, but it felt way too real to be a figment of her imagination. She could even picture her mom saying that to her and what she had been wearing at the time. She remembered that she had been sitting in her mom's lap when this conversation happened. Her mother had disappeared when she was far too young to remember anything, let alone an entire conversation that they had had.

However, she also remembered dreaming of her mother countless times. In those dreams, it looked like she was in hell. Her hair messy, her dress torn. Her face, which was once so beautiful that where ever she went people would stop to look at her, was now ashen and cut in various places; like she was being beaten every day. Those nightmares were probably the reason that she pushed all things related to her childhood aside and suppressed all memories about her. Now that she was trying to remember, it was too far out of reach.

Her brain was telling her not to go there and not to pull out buried memories, but she needed them now. One thing was for damn sure; she was in some deep shit. The kind of shit you never get out of easily, and she needed all the help she could get. Lucille still felt really hot and in pain. She didn't know what was stopping it nor what was making it happen. However, no matter what happened, Lucille knew that she could not give up trying to get out of this mess. She had no control over her body, and she was nowhere near out of pain to do anything physical, but she still had her mind, and it was her only weapon for the time being.

She pressured her brain into remembering whatever it could and she got the same image of her mother. Tattered and rattled beyond recognition, but it was definitely her. She looked starved and was trying to say something to her. Looking at her mother like this, she felt like she was a child again. A helpless child with no mother and no father. Her mother was trying to say something, but all that her brain could remember was the image, and not what she was saying. That made her so fucking angry. Like, why remember it at all, when you are going to cut out the most important part.

Every passing moment being trapped in this fucked up place was worse than before and she had no idea how she would ever get out. She considered the possibility that there might not be a way out of this and she was trapped here for the rest of her life.

That was a fucked up way to go out, not even being in your own body and being killed just because of a rivalry that went back three generations. How the fuck did her grandmother manage to make her life hell from beyond the grave? Pressurizing her brain to remember was just making her mad.

She knew that she had to keep trying to remember what her mother had said in her dreams, but tried to divert her thoughts to something else in the meanwhile. She did not know what to do, so she decided to focus on her surroundings. That was the best she could do right now. She also kept her dreams at the back of her mind, trying to recall what her mother had said, or maybe she had imagined it afterall. 'No! Your mother said it,' she thought to herself. For some reason, she was sure of it. But her memories constantly failed her beyond that one sentence, *"You are strong. Nobody can control you. Remember that. It is of utmost importance. Use the strength you have inside you and overcome the problem you are facing."* This was the only ray of hope that she had right now. She could never let it go. She was absolutely sure that she was going to get out of the mess she had gotten herself into. Maybe she was just deluding herself into thinking that, but she knew that she had no other choice now. She wasn't about to go down without a fight. She had never given in to any hardship in life.

Maybe, this wasn't like any other hardship that she had

faced in life but she couldn't sit around and wait to be rescued. No one was coming to get her. So, it was either this or an eternal abyss, and she seriously did not like the thought of that. She had so much hope and so much anger in that moment, she felt solidified. She looked around and saw a barkeeper standing and looking at her. She was just about to say something, but the moment was gone. Also, she had no idea what the fuck she would say. She considered saying; *'hey, I have been possessed and cannot control my body?'* That was the stupidest thing that she had ever heard and she felt fucking weird even saying it.

Wait…she had just felt solidified again, along with euphoria and anger. Her entire body seemed to have hardened up as waves of anger washed through her, seemingly washing away the now constant pain along with them. In her anger and rage she had completely forgotten to pay attention at that fact. That was an accomplishment. She knew that she had to attain that feeling again. As soon as she said this to herself, she felt searing pain all over. She felt like she was being burned alive.

That made her completely forget everything about trying to take control again and made her focus on this shit show she was in. She tried to calm down, but she could not and the feeling persisted. She yelled out, but her voice sounded like it was reverberating inside her head. Like she was not getting it out. She screamed, *"Please! For the love of God please!*

Fucking stop!" The pain receded a bit, though it was still enough to kill her. But she was not dying. She was very much alive. It was a constant searing sensation, but she could not die. Even though the pain was not yet bearable but it still receded enough for her to focus on what had just happened.

As soon as she had gained control of her body, she had felt the searing pain in her entire body. The only possible reason as to why that could have happened was because she was being stopped from thinking that way again... maybe she was able to break free of the control of whatever the fuck was possessing her and she had been completely free, even if it was just for a second. She knew that she had to achieve that again, but she also knew that if she did she would be subjected to that horrible pain again.

She had never been the kind of person to stop doing something if it got hard, but this was like nothing else anything she had ever experienced before. But it didn't mean that she would change her way of living. She tried once again to gain control of her body but she just could not muster the same energy as before. She remembered that just before breaking free of the witch's control she had felt very angry.

She tried to think about she hated. She thought about her mother, and how she had been deserted. Even though she was living with her aunt and had everything taken care of by her, she still did not feel like she ever got a mother's love. Her aunt had talked to her whenever she needed but she could never replace her mother. She felt like tearing the entire fucking world apart for everything that it had done to her. Just as she was starting to feel angry she felt the pain growing again, but this time around she decided to ignore the pain and just focus on what made her angry. But this was another sort of pain: it was all the years of resentment and emotions she had buried so deep down that they had come to a boiling point and were now bursting forth like a volcano. She still had control of her sight and tried to see what was happening.

She saw that the barkeeper was nowhere near her now and just as she was about to turn around to see where he was she was pulled back and she felt like someone had stabbed her guts. She knew that the pain wasn't real and that she wasn't actually being stabbed but that she was being made to think that it was there. She had always believed in the power of mind over body. She knew that the mind was very powerful and given adverse circumstances it could even go insane as a defense mechanism. Some people had strong minds, and strong wills while others had weak minds, that could be very easily broken.

'I am not one of them!' Lucille thought with all her might.

She thought back to her studies and concluded that this was going on inside her head. She knew that there could be only two reasons that she was not dead yet. The first possibility was that this was all going on inside her head, but that would mean that the pain receptors everywhere would be firing off and her heartbeat would be getting faster and faster until it burst. But that was not happening. The second reason was that she was actually feeling this pain and her heart had already burst. Now, she was just having some fucked up postmortem dream. Both of those explanations did not make any sense whatsoever. If she were to consider the second explanation, why the fuck would her mind even show inside her own mind and make her believe that she had been possessed by a witch. That was just fucking absurd, and her belief that she would probably die due to the insane amount of ridiculousness that went on in her life solidified.

Everything about this just screamed to Lucille that she had gone completely insane. If she were to consider the first explanation; that did give a reason as to why felt pain. However it did not explain why she only felt that pain when she felt a very strong emotion. Both these explanations were fucking retarded and she cursed everything she could think of. This was completely uncharted territory and she knew that it's going to be one hell of a ride trying to make sense of her current predicament.

Even if she were to get out of this fucked up situation she would never be able to tell anyone what she had been through because they would never understand her. She could even be locked up in an insane asylum because that is what happens to people who claim to go through what was happening to her right now. Nobody wants to believe that there is anything other than the normal that we live in, and the world is all sunshine and daisies. However, Lucille had always had firsthand experience with the world being a piece of shit and people just making it worse. People would call her a fool and a liar for even saying that this had happened to her. She would have to keep this buried in her chest until the day she died. She now realized that the pain had almost gone and she was feeling completely fine. She thought about all the people she had treated and she had come heard some pretty fucked up things. She sat across from people who spewed the most senseless shit she had ever heard in her life. Time and time again, she had been reminded that some people could never be treated and all she could do for them was just give them some mind numbing medication so they would at least forget about their pain for a while.

Whenever that realization had hit her through the course of her career, she became surer and surer about one thing. There was no reality of the world. One person's reality could be considered complete lunacy by the people they are surrounded by. Maybe it was because they had been subjected to so much of it that they are never able to recover fully and come back to our mutual reality. They became the outcasts. Lucille knew from firsthand experience that this was a lonely way to live and she would never be able to live like that.

'When I get out of this, nobody will find out about this, EVER!' She knew that even that was a very lonely way to live, however it was much better than the alternative. Once the pain subsided, she decided to at least see what was going on. She saw that she was still sitting inside the bar, but the bartender was nowhere to be seen. She looked around, as much as she could without moving her body, but he was nowhere. She still had no control over her body and could not move around to see anyone.

She had tried that just a while ago and had been subjected to pain yet again. She thought about the bartender and for some reason, felt weird for doing so. She was thinking about some random guy, then suddenly she heard her mother's voice inside her head; *"Go to him."* *'What the actual fuck?'* she thought. She did not know how she knew that it was her mother's voice. There was just this ironclad belief that it was. The voice sounded croaked and weak beyond belief, but it was definitely her. It angered her. This was the moment mother dearest decides to show up, after her life has been fucked up beyond redemption.

She knew that she should have been glad about the fact that her mother was here somewhere, and that she was trying to help her out. But she still hated her for leaving her when she was a child. Lucille had no idea if her mother had left her because she had no other choice and she did not want to think about that right now. *'She was my mother, and it was her job to stick by me side no matter what.'* Lucille thought. Some part of her wanted someone to hold her hand, but another part was like, *'fuck all that!'*

She had been independent for as long as she could remember and did not want to accept any help form anyone. Even when she was living with her aunt, she had asked for the bare minimum and had moved out as soon as she could, which was when she had started training to become a therapist. She didn't want any favors, and she had been repaying her aunt ever since. However, at this moment she knew that she had no choice other than to at least listen to her mother. She had no good ideas of her own that she could put to use, so she decided to give it a shot.

She started to think about the guy and how she could go to him, but it was just way too much. Even trying to think about that made her feel every inch of her had nails pushed through her and that she was being burned alive. *'Well, fuck you mom.*

There you go I tried to give it a shot!' She could not bear the pain any longer and she decided instead that it would be much better use of her mind to think about something else. She realized that she was giving in to the witch's wishes slowly but she did not know what else she could do.

She had tried twice now to break free of the control of the witch and both those times she had been defeated by the witch. She could not even control her body. She had no idea why she was being allowed to even look out of her eyes. Maybe it was just to increase to her suffering so that she could see everything but do nothing about it. She knew that there was no logic to this situation. More than half of the population didn't believe in ghosts or witches or magic or any of that crap. Those who did weren't exactly the kind of people you wanted to be associated with. In other words, they were complete twats.

She had kept her belief in all those things very hidden and had just gone along with the flow of the conversation whenever the topic had been brought up with her colleagues when they dealt with a patient who swore that he was seeing strange things or hearing voices in their head. She had just laughed it off whenever she was asked about her own beliefs regarding the matter. Even though she had separated herself from the younger Lucille who believed in all those things fully, some part of her, a very small part believed that there must be some truth to the stories had mother used to tell her, these things existed.

She had told herself a very convenient story when she had turned sixteen. The same time when her aunt had asked her never to have her palm read. She had managed to convince herself that her mother was a druggie and that her aunt had told her never to get her palm read just so that she could keep up the charade and not ruin the memory Lucille had of her mother. Now, however, she was forced to accept that all these things did, in fact, exist. Not only that but they could have a huge effect on us when they wished.

Her entire life came tumbling down around her. All her life had been spent in a state of semi-belief that her mother, her grandmother and her aunt had been lying to her. She had told herself the simplest story so that she could get out of that and move forward with her life. However, now the truth had been exposed to her in its entirety. She had been shown that everything she dreaded about being an Idona was in fact true and very much life threatening. She had to accept the harder reality that everything she had believed, or at least tried to believe, up until that point had been a lie.

It was kind of like being thrown in the middle of a warzone and being taught how to fire a gun while in the battleground. She had no idea how she was going to battle this… she had no tools. The one slight ray of hope that she thought could get her out of this situation was extinguished almost as soon as it entered her mind. She hoped that if she was found by anyone they would take her to the hospital. However, she then remembered that she had seen a movie where they showed a brain scan of a person that was possessed, and had looked it looked normal.

The person was had been speaking abnormally and showing knowledge of things that they had no way of knowing before. If the only indication of being possessed was that they were suddenly acting weird and they looked like they had been through hell, it was not much to go on. She knew that her mind had been completely exhausted now and she was resorting to making sense of her situation by thinking about what she had seen in movies. That was so pathetic. It was like the reality of the situation kept sinking into her brain.

With every passing moment she was getting more and more scared. She was completely clueless as to how she could bring herself out of this fucking mess. Every test that had been performed looked normal and every medicine they took had no effect on their bodies. She knew that logic had not yet caught up to the paranormal, and probably never would. If all the brain scans were normal and there no abnormal activity, then that would probably mean that whatever was possessing her was keeping her brain performing the exact same functions as it was before. Or it was showing the brain scan of the demon. If that was anywhere near the truth then she was completely fucked.

She was up against a being that was so powerful that it had the capability to manipulate her brain into functioning exactly as it functioned before. She was up against something that she could never even hope to defeat without outside help. She remembered her mother's words, *'Go to him.'* She had no idea how that would even help her but that was all that she had to go on. She could only hope that he would get her out of this situation, even though it would be a foolish to hope that. The possibility that her mind was making all of this up just as a defense mechanism was very real. She thought about how her life gone up until that point and she realized that it probably was. However she had no other choice. Suddenly, she remembered that it was not a demon possessing her; rather, it was a witch. It was in fact, the same witch that her mother had warned her of a very long time ago. 'Lumis Ash,' she remembered the words she heard before her body was taken from her. She had gone into the fortune teller's camp and had just sat down. The fortune teller had asked to see her hand and then doubled over, her voice completely changing into a raspy snarl that shook her to her core.

It was not a petite voice, like when she was talking normally, rather it sounded like sand paper was being rubbed against concrete; raspy, ugly fucking voice. But when it changed, it was like the voice of an old woman who had grown accustomed to being ruthless. Like the voice of an old bitch who was destroying her life. Lucy concluded that it was none other than Lumis Ash. Well, that and the fact that she had said that her name was Lumis Ash. She had said that she had been waiting a long time for this to happen.

What did that mean? Had she been waiting for her to go to a fortune teller? Is that what she meant? Why would she do that? Her aunt had told her that there was a curse placed on her that made sure that if she ever went to a fortune teller, something bad was going to happen. What could possibly have happened that she had a curse this specific placed on her? What the fuck kind of a witch has a rivalry and thinks, *'You know what! If this's bitch's great granddaughter ever goes to a fortune teller, I'm going to fuck her life up.'* That was just beyond absurd. Suddenly she had a thought. She remembered the story that her mother had told her the night she had disappeared. There was a castle near where grandmother had lived; Landsend or some fucked up name. Her mother had told her that that was where the witch had lived. So maybe, just maybe, the witch was bound to the castle somehow and could only leave if she had a body to possess. She knew that all this had no use. She could contemplate all she wanted to, but in the end, the bottom line was still that she was in a situation that she had no way out of.

However, she had found out through years of treating patient after patient that if you kept thinking about a problem a solution will present itself one way or the other. All of this seemed good in theory, however, all of this was still speculation. Even if her train of thought was true and the witch was bound to the castle somehow, she had no idea why she was being subjected to this. It couldn't just be because of a spat that took place god knows when. Even if Lucy considered the possibility that she was special and that the witch could only possess her that would not be true.

She had possessed the fortune teller right in front of her. This made her even madder. This bitch was actually seeking Lucille out to make her life miserable. She had a constant sense of regret and the only life line was a man who was a stranger. She had no idea why her mother's voice had told her to go to him. But she knew that it was her mother who had spoken to her, into her head, somehow, which completely made no sense. Lucille was sure that she was trapped in her own being; in her own mind. So how could her mother speak to her when she was trapped in her own mind? This was verging on the stranger territory of telekinesis. She had no idea if her mother was dead or if she was a prisoner somewhere. But she knew that even a witch could not hoodwink her into thinking that her mother had spoken to her. She did not know how she was so sure of this but just that she was. Even if she thought about it logically, it made sense. Why would the witch give her advice to go to a man who could rescue her? If the witch wanted Lucy to meet the guy then she would have just led her to the bar so that it happened on its own.

Lucy knew that she was convincing herself... she had no idea how the witch thought and was just deluding herself into thinking that, but she knew that she had to give it a shot. In a nutshell, if she was so sure that it was her mother that had spoken to her, then it must have been her mother. She was thinking based purely on instinct, and even though she had made up her mind; that she was now going to think logically, there was no way that she could make sense out of this. So, now all that was left were just hunches and guesses, and she was doing exactly that. Up until now, she had drawn the conclusion that Lumis could not leave her castle, without possessing her.

Even though that was logically flawed she still knew that there had to be a reason that she was being subjected to this. Lucy refused to believe that all this was happening just because her great grandmother had got in a spat with the witch. The second conclusion was; she could only take control of her body if she felt a really strong emotion, even if that meant that she would be subjected to an unbearable pain. If the witch was so powerful then why the fuck did it even let Lucy know that she had been possessed? But what caught her attention the most was the fact that her mother was speaking to her now, even if it was just one sentence, she was speaking to her. She remembered her mother's voice and felt like crying. It was not at all how she remembered it to be. It was so weak and so pathetic that it sounded like she had been beaten and battered for every day since she had gone missing. Lucy now felt pity for her mother, instead of just the blind anger she once felt.

Now that she was in this situation herself, she could entertain the possibility that her mother could have actually gone through a lot, which sort of justified her disappearance and abandonment of her only daughter. Even after that it had been made sure that Lucy was taken care of. She completely believed now that her mother was speaking to her from somewhere, telling him to go to the stranger. Presumably because he would get her out of the shit show she was in. The only way she had been able to get control of her body was to feel a really strong emotion. Since her life was not exactly filled with happiness she did not know how to summon that emotion.

There was only regret, anger, desolation, and an insatiable

thirst to prove herself. Right now, she had no idea how to feel that strongly again and the pain she had felt after that was far too excruciating for her to think like that again. Another thought struck her mind, with blinding clarity. Wait! That was it; her mother was speaking to her again. Her mother had just told her to *'Go to him'*. She had been thinking all this while about herself and not about the one person who could supposedly save her. She had to think about him. She tried to focus on that, trying her best to think of him. She just had a momentary glance of his face, so she was having a hard time remembering what he looked like, which was very weird since she was really good with faces. His face, however, kept on flicking in and out of her mind. His face was morphing into other images of the people she knew. One moment it was his face and the next, it changed into the face of her first boyfriend, and the next it was the face of her first crush and then, it was just an animal. His jawline was changing, and the shape of his eyes was altering. She knew that that was impossible, no matter what happened, Lucille always had razor sharp focus and she was always the kind of person who would never be distracted, no matter what.

The only possible explanation was that the witch was playing with her mind. There could be no other reason why this could be happening. This made her even surer that it had been her mother who had talked to her and that the guy she had told her to go to was her salvation. She tried with all her might to get a grip of herself, and struggled to remember the exact moment she saw him. She was thinking that she was going to get herself free of this shit show, that, no matter what, she would not give up fighting and there was not a fucking chance that she would let the witch win. Just trying to remember his face and the exact moment she saw him made her feel elated. *'Wow… even the happy memories I am making is in this fucked up place.'*

She thought, and laughed. That hunch, or maybe it was laugh, did the trick. She had solidified back into her body, and was in the moment when she saw him. She looked around, hoping to see him. She tried to freeze that image into her mind. She thought that if she did this, then she would be able to focus on his image. She succeeded; it was a pure hunch and it totally worked. She felt elated at that thought and just for a moment, got another feeling of being solidified. She looked around and saw that she was still sitting in the bar and she felt the same feeling of being burned alive again.

"What the fuck?! Fucking stop please," she screamed internally once more. It did not stop. The pain was not receding. She was just being burned alive and she lost all consciousness, but the silver lining, although bleak and blurred was that she still kept the same image in her mind. The image

of the man that was to save her. Even though she was asleep, her mind kept on working. Being a therapist she did have some knowledge about how the brain worked, and she knew that maybe she was just in a deeper part of her brain.

She had worked herself up so much that even after losing consciousness she was still thinking, albeit in a dream form. In her dream, she kept on looking at his face, so much so that she actually memorized it. He was unbelievably handsome and very lean. She remembered his eyes and his jawline, his deep, dark eyes and razor sharp jawline. Everything about him was etched into her heart. She realized that she was thinking. If she was thinking, then maybe she was conscious; although she had no idea on how to confirm that.

She just knew that she had to take what she could get and right now, she was not in pain anymore and she could picture him in her mind. She was trying to visualize what he looked like and what he sounded like. She imagined that he had a deep, gravelly voice. Basically, she was trying to recall and make up, as accurately as she could, as much as she could about him; how he walked, how he would handle different types of customers at bars, and more. She imagined him being with her, the linchpin to her situation, and her saving grace. She did not want to be the damsel in distress, but it did not look like she had much of a choice right now.

That thought made her feel a surge of anger. Anger the likes of which she had never felt before. She wanted to fucking rip this whole world a new asshole, but she was not even able to get out of this mess. All of these emotions coupled together were enough to make her whole once more. She was once again solidified and this time, she did not feel pain. She felt like herself again, but where the fuck was she...she was sitting in the back of a car. She looked at the driver, and it was the same guy from the bar. She could not fucking believe it. She saw him look in the back mirror and catch her eye. After a pause, while the shock settled in, she said, *"Turn around."* And then, the car crashed.

Chapter 5
The White Bird

James wanted to go as far away from everyone as possible. He was just about done with the life that he had led up until that point and all he wanted to feel now was some peace and quiet. Four days; that was all that it took for this to happen. He had gone into work thinking that it was just going to be a regular day and that he would be facing the same problems as usual. That being said, all that he had expected to encounter were rowdy assholes, the lazy bartenders, his asshole boss, great tips, and hot babes.

How was he to know that his whole life would be taking a U-turn and giving it to him straight up the ass? Ever since that day he had completely shut himself from the world and had had no contact with anyone except for Harry. He was sure that his boss would be begging him by now to come back, but he had no intention whatsoever of going back. The frustrating part was that even though he had no intention of going back to the bar he had no idea what he did want to do.

The indecisiveness made him mad, because all he was doing was just wasting away day after day. He spent all his day just thinking about that girl from the bar. He had no idea that just two glances could affect him so much. The weirdest part was that his obsession was completely unprecedented. He always knew when to call it quits and never dragged anything on when it was finished. He had no idea who the girl was, no idea where he could find her again; he was also fairly sure that she was not local to the area so she would not be frequenting the bar anytime soon. He had no idea how he could track her down and even if he could what the fuck would he even say. *'Hey, remember me? I saw you at the bar and haven't been able to stop thinking about you since then. Wanna hang out sometime?'* This wasn't exactly the best opening line.

Just a few days ago, he was just dealing two of his regulars and then he looked around and saw the most regal looking girl that he had ever laid his eyes on. She was the most magical and breathtaking creature that had ever laid in his eyes. It seemed as if she was drawing him towards herself. James wondered what was it about her that was drawing him so much that he was unable to even function properly. He hadn't been able to stop thinking about her.

He tried to remember her face exactly as he had seen it in the bar. She looked trapped and desolate. He didn't know why he got that feeling; just that he did. Maybe that was the entire reason that he was drawn to her; she was just like him. He could feel that she was calling out to him, drawing him in, closer and closer, needing him to come rescue her, made so much more apparent by the fact that he had seen her sitting in his backseat calling him to turn back towards her. That was something that he felt was the case, in hindsight.

However, he was sure that that was absolutely true. He had been so selfish, turning away like that. He should have gone back to her, even if everything about her turned out to be false, at least, he would have the satisfaction of knowing that it was false. At least then he wouldn't be in this fucked up state of mind. He regretted his actions so much. That day, in that moment, if he could do it over again, he would definitely choose to go to her. He wouldn't have left, he wouldn't have run away. He would have talked to her, he was sure that she needed him, to do what... that he didn't know. He just knew that he had to find her.

With that thought in his mind he got out of his bed. He was tired of the feeling of helplessness and desolation he felt all the time. He wanted to actually do something about finding her. James was a very resourceful person and when he set his mind to something, more often than not, he actually ended up accomplishing it. So he called up Harry and asked him to come over to his place. *"I am going to find her."* James said, and for the first time in so many days he was actually feeling hopeful. As if he was on the right path. He felt a modicum of satisfaction being in action. *"Oh… 'kay?"* Harry said.

He knew who James was talking about but he just couldn't bring himself to be even slightly excited about that. He had seen his friend get hurt so many times that he really didn't want James to get hurt again. Although, he knew that there was no way that he would be able to stop him. James just nodded and looked at him excitedly, pulling out his cell. *"How are you going to find her?"* Harry asked. He knew everything about James's wealth and was sure that James would do just about everything he could to find her. *"Well I don't have anything about her. I don't have her picture… nothing really. So I am going to go back to the bar and get the video footage from the day she came into the bar. Then I am going to set a private investigator on her tail. They are probably going to find her. When they do. I am going to casually show up where she is and talk to her."* He said. *"Sooo… you are doing all of this just to get in her pants?"* he asked. Harry knew very well that this wasn't the case, but he wanted to find another way for this to end.

He thought, maybe if he was able to convince his friend not to repeat his past mistakes, James would change for the better. *"I don't know, Harry."* James said, looking thoughtful. *"For the weirdest reason, I just know that she is the one… or maybe that she just needs me. I don't know what the fuck is going on but I do know that I have to find her… and find her, I will,"* he said, looking Harry dead in the eyes. *"Let's go to the bar then."*

Harry said. Seeing the passion igniting once again in James's eyes, Harry knew that it would be worse than useless to even try and convince James to give up on this fool's quest and live out his life. He was being toyed with and Harry didn't like that. However, he had accepted it. Some people were just doomed to repeat an eternity doing the same thing. Both of them went to the bar, where they were greeted by James's boss, who was just coming in with his jackass of a girlfriend. *"Oh, look who we have here!"* He said trying to sound even cockier than he usually was, perhaps because his girlfriend was with him. *"I thought you wouldn't be coming in from now on."*

"I am not. I just have to get something and then I'm gone." James replied to his boss's utter displeasure. He knew that leaving just like that and going MIA would have caused his boss a lot of grief the past couple of days, but he didn't give a single solitary fuck about that. *"Then you aren't allowed in. Fuck off,"* his boss replied and James smiled. He had been looking forward to this. *"Oh… well that's unfortunate. What are we going to do now, Harry?"* James said sarcastically. The guards standing on the gates of the bar smirked at James. He was way more popular with all of the employees than his boss

was and James knew that this jerk wouldn't be able to stop him.

"If you step a foot inside this bar, I will have you arrested!" his boss said, trying to look as intimidating as he could. For a man who was just five-seven, his boss sure did have a lot of balls. What he lacked for in height and brains, he more than made up for being absolute scum of the planet. *"Try and stop me."* James said quietly and then walked on into the bar. He could hear his boss yelling at the guards to stop him and the guards trying to calm him down.

James walked into the security room and found just the guy he was looking for. *"Mark! How ya doing, bruv?"* James exclaimed. Mark was one of the guys who knew about James's wealth, after James had asked him some unusual favors. He was an absolute genius when it came to technology and could do just about anything sitting behind his desk with a computer that robbers could with guns labored to do. Nobody knew why he was even working here. According to Mark he was just passing time, living the good life.

"Why the fuck have you not left your apartment for the past week?" he asked. James tried to guess how the fuck he even knew that. *"Let me guess, you've been keeping an eye on the lobby monitors in my building?"* he asked. *"Do you really think I have nothing better to do in my life?"* Mark replied

sarcastically. *"I just hacked the street camera around your place and it came up with a hit just now,"* he smiled as if that was just something that people do. *"Using government assets to keep an eye on me. I'm flattered."* James replied. *"But I need you to do something for me."* He said, getting down to business. James really didn't want to waste another second wasting his time.

"Anything. What can I do for you?" Mark asked, immediately letting go of the sarcastic tone that he had been using to talk to James. James appreciated that about Mark. When it came to being professional, Mark was the best. James had a sneaking suspicion that Mark was ex-intelligence but he never brought that up with him. As long as what James wanted was done, he was good. *"I need you to pull of the footage of the last day I was working here. The camera above the bartenders."* James said.

"Oh… Well tough luck man. The cameras were down that day. Maintenance issues." Mark replied. *"Who are you looking for?"* he asked. He could sense that James was very serious about this and wanted to do all he could to help him out. *"Then pull up the footage from the neighbors."* James said, ignoring Mark's question. He had no intention of letting anyone but Harry know what was going on. It wasn't as if James was ashamed about wanting to find the girl, he just didn't want to

answer any more questions than was necessary.

Mark nodded and got to work. Within a couple of short questions he had gotten access to the neighboring shops' cameras and they were all looking at the video footage. James noticed the time stamp and asked Mark to fast forward to when he anticipated that the girl would go in the bar. Mark kept fast forwarding till the time James saw himself get out of the bar and rush off to his car. There was no sign of the girl coming in or going out whatsoever. James stood, staring flabbergasted at the computer screen. He asked Mark to start the footage again, and then again and then again but there was no sign that the girl had come in or gone out.

He wondered how the fuck that was possible. He was sure that he had not made the girl up in his mind, because Charlie and Roy had seen her too. *"Where is she?"* Harry asked in an undertone. He looked at James with the concern of a parent looking at their hungover child. James knew that he was making a fool of himself and even Mark looked concernedly at him. *"Just… rewind the footage one more time."* James said and Mark looked at Harry. They shared a silent message and Mark said, *"Why don't we look at some of the other cameras?"*

He started to pull up the cameras at the street corner and they went over the footage again and again but there was still no sign of her. James had no other choice but to entertain the possibility that he had just made up the girl in his head. He also knew that there was only one way to confirm that his mind wasn't playing tricks on him. He went out of the security room, both Mark and Harry following him. He knew that there were only two other people who could confirm that she was actually there. James wondered if he had been drugged which caused him to hallucinate everything that had happened that day. His belief that he had actually seen her wavered just a bit. He knew that the chances of him actually having been drugged were very low, because he hadn't even drank anything or eaten anything that day but the situation was playing itself out to make him look like a retard. James saw that Charlie and Roy had come in and were, as usual, sitting in their regular spot and eating their regular shitty burgers.

Why the fuck they even came to this bar was beyond James... these guys were bleeding rich. *"Hey, Charlie, Roy!"* James called out. Both of them looked behind and yelled! *"Jamey boy!"* James smiled. He was in no mood for their shit and immediately got down to business. *"Hey, remember when I was in the bar the last time?"* He said. *"Yea what about that?"* Roy said. Even they understood that James was very serious right now and by the foreboding looks of Harry and the Mark behind him, they knew that they would get their asses handed to them if they fucked around. *"The girl sitting in the stool. Remember her?"* He asked.

"The hot one. Yea we do." Charlie replied. All of them had gone crazy for her. James nodded and turned to look at Harry, who was looking at James with a look of concern and pity. *"See, I told you."* James said. *"Well, why the fuck isn't she showing up in any of the cameras?"* Mark said. He wasn't used to being the one without answers. He would have found her but he had practically nothing to go on... unless, *"James, do you remember her face?"* he asked.

"Yea, I do. Why?" James asked. Just as he said this, he felt his memory of her slipping out of his mind once again. He couldn't understand how the fuck that was possible. *"Well, if you describe her to me, I could run a facial recognition software on her, see what comes up?"* he suggested. James knew that Mark would do just about anything to help him out, but he wasn't sure if he would be able to describe her. He couldn't even remember exactly what she looked like by now, but he decided to give it a chance nonetheless.

All of them went back to the security room, including Charlie and Roy, whom James wanted to come with. Charlie fired up his desktop once again and started asking James questions about how she looked. With each question he asked it became more and more difficult to describe her. Throughout the questions that Mark asked, Charlie and Roy sat quietly and when the sketch was finally finished, both of them looked at

James. *"She looked nothing like that, bro,"* they said. Mark looked at them and then back at James.

"What do you wanna do here, Jamey boy?" he asked sounding excited at the prospect of finally seeing this mystery girl who was so hard to find. *"Run it through facial recognition. Let's see what comes up,"* he said. All the possible matches that turned up looked nothing like the girl he saw sitting at the bar that day and both Charlie and Roy just kept on murmuring, *'said so.'* *"Why don't you guys describe her to Mark?"* he said. They started telling their version of what she looked like, which was a complete waste of time because even those matches didn't turn anything up.

Finally, James had enough. He got up, enraged, his blood pumping hard in his entire body and punched the wall. The wall cracked. Charlie and Roy winced at that and looked apologetically at James. *"We're sorry, bruv. That is exactly how I remember her to be."* Charlie said, and Roy nodded. *"Get out,"* James said quietly. He knew that his anger towards both of them was unfair and he probably shouldn't have said that, but he didn't care. *"James, maybe it's time to give up on this,"* Harry suggested timidly. Even though they had wasted a good ten hours in the bar, never once had the thought of quitting crossed James's mind.

"No," James said. He knew that this was a complete bust

and he would never find her like that. *"I'm leaving."* *"James, you are looking for a ghost."* Mark said. *"Look, I know that this must be important to you. Can you guess anything about her?"* he asked. *"Like what?"* He asked. *"Did she look to be military?"* Mark asked and once again the suspicion that Mark was ex-intelligence rose in his mind. *"She didn't look to be particularly tough... no I am sure she was just a normal citizen."* James replied. He didn't know why he said that, but there was nothing that he remembered from her mannerisms that suggested anything remotely government about her.

"Okay, how about this?" Mark said, looking at the monitor screen. He seemed to be considering what he was about to say. *"How about I run all the sketches you gave me through military databases? That way, if she is ex-military, or if she is serving... or if she is undercover, or if she is intelligence, we will know about her. If anything turns up, I'll give you a call or send a text with the words, 'banana peel'."* He knew that his suggestion could land him in a lot of trouble, however he was prepared to do that if that meant helping James out. Mark knew everything about James, and it was a very good thing to have a man like James on his side.

"Yea... why don't you do that?" James agreed distractedly. It had come to the point where he was considering another idea altogether. He was sure that even the military or intelligence

databases would not turn up anything He thought that he would much rather just go out on his own and try to find her. With that thought in mind, James said his goodbyes to Harry and Mark and left the bar to go and look for her. He had no particular destination in mind, nor did he know what he would do, once he did find her. He just knew that he had to find her, one way or the other.

That plan was going about as good as could have been expected at that time. James had been driving aimlessly through the country. James wasn't a mythical person, he didn't really believe in life after death, and he sure as hell didn't think much about anything. However, he knew that this situation was different than anything he had faced in life. He still couldn't wrap his mind around how the girl had managed to evade all surveillance but Charlie and Roy still remembered her. He wasn't at all a person who believed any sort of supernatural crap. On the contrary, he was quite the opposite. He was more of a 'in the moment' kind of a person. Where if he wanted to do something, he would just do it, no second thoughts, and no fucks given. However, he knew that there was something going on here that he wasn't fully able to grasp. He wasn't sure if that meant that it was supernatural or anything like that. Even if that were the case, which James was sure was not, he did not give a fuck. He would find her if that was the last thing he ever did.

Being the kind of person he was, James had ignored all the calls he had gotten from Harry. He knew that Harry would want to tag along, but that would just fuck James's internal compass up. Harry had even gone as far as to call James through Mark's phone, which he picked up. *"Hey, don't you dare fucking hang up!"* Harry said, as soon as James picked up. James was in no mood to talk to anyone at the moment, however Harry didn't deserve that. *"Hey Harry,"* James said glumly.

"Where in the fuck are you?" Harry asked him. James knew that Harry had probably asked Mark to find James, but he had refused. Mark was very loyal to James, and since Harry was James's best friend, Mark had let him use his phone to call James. *"I can't tell you that, buddy."* He replied. James wanted to hang up but what Harry said next stopped him. *"James…"* Harry began very seriously, *"are you sure you want to do this alone?"* he asked. James thought he was about to hear another one of Harry's lectures and did not fancy that at all. He would have hung up right away if it hadn't been for his tone of voice.

"Yes, Harry," James said, equally seriously. He had never been surer about anything in his life than he was about this. *"Okay, then. Call me if you need me, please."* Harry said with an air of finality in his voice and hung up. He knew that Harry would mind that he was being such a stubborn jackass. James

had a very good reason for avoiding Harry's calls for as long as he had done. He knew that Harry would be looking for ways to proceed logically and James had wasted ten hours doing that, but to no avail. So right now, what he wanted to do was do something irrational.

Something that just didn't just make sense, like that girl's disappearance didn't make sense either.Now while driving, he had let his hands go on autopilot and he had twisted, turned, gone around just about everywhere he could have thought about and yet, he still didn't feel right. It was as if he knew that there was some place that he needed to be at, but he didn't know where that was or how he was going to find that place. His best hope was that he would just find it eventually.

He didn't really have much going on in his life that he had to look back to at his home. However, he reasoned, if he found this girl, there was something to look forward to. If Harry had known what was going on in James's mind, he would have suggested a complete restart. He would have told him that looking for this girl was a fool's quest and that he was just wasting himself away behind her. James knew that if he wished, he could pack up and be gone in an hour, he was able to afford that quite easily. But one thought held him back from doing so; he had no one to share it with.

What was the use of having all of this wealth if he was

going to be spending it alone for the rest of his life? He had been lonely most of his life and now, even thinking about getting back together with his ex-girlfriend was unbearable. It was as if he was somehow betraying the girl at the bar. James, deep down at heart, was a family man. He wanted to find a girl and settle down. However, all the girls he had met and been with, had none of the qualities he was looking for. Even all the girls he had fucked in the bar were just because of his carnal desire. There were no strings attached and he made sure that both of them knew it.

But this girl, he didn't even know her name, but she had some sort of power over him. He knew that he was being drawn towards her. He knew that there was something so different in her than all the other girls that he had met in his life, that he couldn't even begin to describe that. The way she had made him so damn hard with just one look, the way he felt inside his heart about her, he knew that that feeling was alien to him. He had never felt that way about anyone or anything. He knew that if Harry were here he would say that he was just using his dick instead of his brains, but he knew that he was not.

He was following his heart. He knew the reason that Harry disapproved of his actions, was because he thought that James wanted to get into that girl pants – that was not false completely. However, what he failed to understand was that there should be practicality in a relationship. He was attracted to her, not just because he craved her sexually, but he also longed for her through his heart. He wanted to love her, but he didn't know how the fuck he was even going to do that.

The odds stacked up against him were so tall that his chances didn't even seem slim, they were just non-existent. He was just driving around aimlessly, no idea where he was going, and this was after he had jerked off in bed, thinking about her, for an entire week. He was weak for her and he couldn't remember the last time, if ever, a person had made him feel that way. He knew that eventually he would find her, no matter how many strings he had to pull, or how many people he had to pay off. Harry was a part of James' life, maybe he was an annoying part, but he was a part for damn sure. They were together for better or for worse.

The fact that Harry finally gave into his pursuit of the girl, was a testament to how serious he was when it came to caring about what James thought. Searching for her felt painful. Just one glimpse made him feel like that was just about it. He would give anything to see her or find out something about her. He knew that even if he managed to find out her name; that would be more than enough to locate her; all he would have to do then was get her number and then have it traced. But that was the thing, he had no idea how he was supposed to go after her.

So he had decided to follow his instincts and just go with his guts. He was still driving around in his G-Wagon and he realized that he had been to this place before. These were the towering cliffs in Cornwall. He could see the waves smashing against the rocks down below, and the whole place seemed to be stuck in time. He looked at the horizon, and as much as he looked at it, he realized that the entire place was doomed to repeat that exact moment for all of eternity. The sky cast a foreboding grey glow over everything in sight and the water looked like it would kill you if you stepped a toe in it. He wondered how that would feel, to do the same thing over and over again, all his life. It was amazingly beautiful, in the cruelest way he could imagine. For some weird reason he could relate to the feeling of being stuck in time and doomed to repeat his life over and over again. That was a beautiful experience in and of itself. Standing above the waves, hearing it roar into his ears, gazing at it as it smashed into the rocks, trying desperately to reach up towards James, just so it could suck him into the abyss.

James related to the waves and sympathized with it. He knew that not most people would see it that way and that they preferred the sea to be calm. He however, preferred it wild and unleashed. On that particular day, it felt as if that was exactly what the sea wanted to be. It was battering relentlessly against the cliffs, so hard that he could almost feel the water jumping up to him, calling out to him, inviting him in. James felt the weirdest urge to jump into the water and end it all right then and there. He loathed feeling the way he did, anxious and desperate. But at the same time, he loved it.

He wondered if he should feel scared, but he didn't. He knew that he was here because he was meant to be here, not because he was wandering. He was at Land's End cliff and they looked so familiar. He, however, couldn't remember when he came here. He knew that there was something wrong with his memory. He just seemed to remember things and forget them at will; like an entire chapter or segments of his life, just vanished. He had himself tested but the results came back clear showing that there was nothing wrong with him. He was absolutely healthy and there was nothing wrong with his mind, but he couldn't understand why he was forgetting such huge chunks of his life. The doctor suggested that he try some memorizing exercises and did try them and he aced all of the tests, leaving the doctors baffled. They couldn't seem to figure out why he wasn't able to remember his childhood or memories. Then he just gave up when they suggested some off the books therapies. Just one of the perks of being rich, James guessed.

People go fucking crazy to do what you want, just so they could call it in someday. He didn't want to do that. He was fine with the way things were, just a bit curious. Just like he was curious now as to when the fuck he had been on these cliffs. He wanted to know that and he got out of his car and sat down on one of the boulders. The fresh sea air hitting his face playfully and making his hair messy. He ran his fingers through his hair and neatly pulled his hair away from his face.

He was glad for the fresh sea air. He had his air conditioning off for a couple of days now and only stopped to get food or pulled off at some cheap motel or whatever was available to sleep for the night. That was why he had been able to cross such a great distance in a couple of days. He had been driving non-stop and rather than feeling tired or exhausted, he felt rejuvenated. He felt great and now it was as if the fresh air was making him even more powerful. He was able to think clearly for the first time and he thought about what he was doing.

He had just driven right from his home miles across the country and was now in pursuit of a woman whom he didn't even know the name of. He didn't know how he had gotten here, the previous couple of days had been a bit fuzzy, and he was just sitting here now. He had no idea what he was supposed to do now, though he was enjoying himself immensely. The air blowing harder and harder still and with each crashing wave, his thoughts became clearer. He saw the girl in his bar, and in pursuit of her he had gone across the country. What the fuck kind of logic was that?

He was supposed to be the one who could think clearly. Just as he was thinking this his heart yearned for him to be with her. It was a battle between the heart and mind. His mind was telling him to go back to his home, but his heart was telling him to go on. He didn't know who to listen to, his mind was making sense and he knew he had to return home. He enjoyed the air for a bit more and then got up to walk to his car. Just as he was about to get into his car, the sounds of the waves crashing and the wind blowing became dead silent, and through the silence cut the voice of a nightingale.

It was singing and it was a song like no other he had listened to. It was a melody about love, sex, romance, and just plain sorrow. James didn't know how all of that tied into each other, but those were all the raw emotions that he felt when he was listening to that song. He didn't know how long he stood there for, or how long he listened to the song. He just knew that he was swaying to the music and it was arousing him. All he could picture was that girl in his mind, like he had done a thousand times before except this time, it was as if it was a dream.

He wasn't consciously making this up; it was as if he was in a dream. He felt like this was all just happening to him. He was lying in bed with her, and he could picture her perfectly. Her perfect body on top of his, and they were making out. It felt absolutely perfect; her lips as soft as he could imagine and she smelled like an orchard. Just absolutely perfect. She removed her lips from his and took off her shirt and pants. She wasn't wearing any underwear and was now entirely nude, standing in front of him with her arms hanging loosely by her side.

The sight of her perfect body was enough to make him jump on top of her, but years of experience had taught him that that would be a bad move. He was waiting for her to get back on top of him and said, *"What's wrong, babe?"* *"I'm not here, the time for us to be together is not now. Your lover is gone,"* she said. His vision was absolutely destroyed and he was standing back again at the cliffs, completely soaked in sweat, among other things.

Chapter 6
The Beach

James stood atop the cliff and looked at his car. He couldn't hear the nightingale sing now. It was like the only reason that the nightingale had sung was so that it could tell him what awaited him if he succeeded in his quest to find the girl. He was now in a bit of dilemma. The chain of events since that day at the bar had made him less and less sure that this was just an obsession to find her. It was more like his destiny. He knew that normal people didn't just go around hearing nightingales and getting visions of some girl they had met just once. However, he could not understand one thing; how was it possible that this was happening to him.

James's life hadn't exactly been normal… but this was above and beyond what was considered abnormal. It was downright magical… a sinister, evil magic that had bound him to her and left him a slave to the single desire to find her. He hadn't eaten, slept or done anything to sustain his body. He just kept on pushing; harder and harder so that he could find the girl. This meant so much more to him than just wanting to be in a relationship with this girl, being able to kiss her, make love to her, and make her feel like the queen of the world. This was about something else, something much deeper was at play here.

He had hid his wealth from other girls, so they could prove to him that they were worthy of his love, that they weren't with him just because he was rich. But with this girl, he knew already that she was the one. She was his, and she wouldn't be like any of the other girls he had met. That was a very rare feeling for James. He had gone his entire life alone, without the support of any loved ones, with almost no one to rely on. His life was just one moment after the next, breathing, eating, and sleeping; nothing remotely beyond normal.

All his life, he had craved companionship of a woman and he had gone to great lengths to acquire it. He knew that if he were just to show a single hint of how rich he was he would be have a cavalcade of women throwing themselves at him. And a small part of him wanted that kind of security in a relationship. But deep down, he knew that that was the most disgusting form of a relationship. He knew that if he were to be in that kind of a relationship someday, someone richer would come along and she would be gone. Even though he had fucked a lot of women, he never cheated on his last girlfriend.

This time around though, he was now sure that something supernatural was at work here. He could not think of any other reason as to why the nightingale had chosen that exact moment to start singing, nor did he know why that song had transformed into a vision of her standing naked in front of him, giving him a message. He could have passed it off as a hallucination, but he knew that that wasn't true, and it wouldn't make any sense either. He was not about to just let all the weird things happening to him slide by just for the sake of convenience and call them hallucinations.

If the reality of the situation was that something supernatural was going on, then, he would gladly accept that. Yet, he had to consider everything before doing taking a step. He couldn't just let happen all that had happened and leave any thought unfinished. If it was, why was there a message there? Why wasn't it just plain sex? If it were a hallucination then that would have revealed his deepest desire, which was to be with her; close to her in every way possible. But that hadn't happened in his vision. He had dreamt that she was giving him a message for him to come closer to her and to find her.

He hadn't even come in his pants, but he was sure that if it was his brain doing this, he would have come. That's the way it was, the way wet dreams worked. He could have passed it off for a wet dream but he didn't feel the desire to masturbate, nor did he feel sexual in any way. In fact, he felt quite the opposite. He felt concerned about the girl. He felt as if she was far out of his reach, and was slowly but surely slipping away further and further. He could not let that happen, but he had no idea what he was supposed to do.

He felt as if he had been given a mission, without being told what the mission was. He was just given the objective of the mission, which was to find her but he didn't know how he was supposed to do that. Immediately his mind came up with a simple answer. He was in this situation because of his sub conscious mind had chosen a girl and made that girl his entire world. Now, he would have to follow his instincts to get to her. He was already doing that but this time along, it was different.

He understood how a mind works. He knew that this level of attachment and love could not be formed over such a small period of time. Those decisions were made by the sub conscious mind were the ones which were made based on facts that were impossible for the conscious mind to pick up. So, being much faster than the conscious mind, it made those decisions, which was his instincts. That was what made James so sure that she was so different than all the other girls out there. The feelings that James had for this girl were not those which a conscious mind could make. The only thing left to do now was to follow his instincts.

He got in his car and started driving away from the cliffs. He knew that he would have to follow his instincts. But now that his instincts had realized that he was depending on them to make his decisions, they stubbornly refused to work. He was trying to think what his next move was going to be, but he could just not make a spontaneous decision. He knew that now he would not be able to do that, so the only thing that was left to be done was to give his sub conscious mind to rest and think about it. So he pulled over and tried to sleep.

However the only thing that was in his mind was just how beautiful that girl looked. He kept on imagining her until his mind got diverted thinking about the logistics of the situation. He tried to consider the worst possibility i.e. what if he couldn't find her. Immediately, he felt like he was being suffocated. He had never been claustrophobic, nor had he ever been, however, he felt as if the walls were closing in. James tried to get a grip on himself. He now knew that that was not a possibility at all, now.

He had always been able to control his thoughts pretty well and he knew that he needed to throw out the thread of self-doubt that festered deep in his mind. He knew that his heart was damn sure that he was going to find her, but his mind felt a bit differently about the situation. It wasn't as if his mind was telling him that it was a foolish decision going after her but he just felt as if he was missing something. As if he had everything he could hope for to get to her but he refused to recognize that. Somehow, it all felt blocked. It didn't feel supernatural this time along, however, it felt like he wasn't ready to know it all.

James knew that he couldn't do anything about it right now. So he decided to think about what he did know. He remembered thinking that there was something supernatural going on here. He tried to remember the first time that he had seen the ghoul in his back mirror. How the fuck was that possible? He had immediately crashed the car in the sidewalk and gotten out. He had been sick for a week following that. He had heard things about people being possessed and the people surrounding those people seeing apparitions and hearing weird voices.

He did not believe any of that shit for even a second but now the situation was so different. He had seen movies and in those that all had been solved an exorcism, but he never trusted that up until this point. He thought that in those myths, there could be a faint glimmer of hope for him actually being with his true love. The possibility that she could be possessed was very much possible now. That was the only way he could make sense of all that had happened up until this point.

In essence, James was ready to consider every possible explanation of what was happening to him. The constant weird occurrences and the visions that he had, along with the apparitions, left him no other conclusion to draw. James was the kind of person who would go along with the flow of things. He was not the kind to get scared; any normal person would have been scared out of their minds, but not James. Even now he was thinking about everything objectively. He thought about where this was all leading… and if it came to where he thought it was going to come down to, he would have to pull out some pretty huge guns.

He didn't know if he would have to fight for her or do some weird sacrificial shit. But he was ready to do anything to get her back. He knew that nothing was off the table when it came to getting her back. With all the thoughts about her festering in his mind, he went to sleep. His dreams were very weird that night. James dreamt that he was in a forest. It looked so real that he actually felt everything around him. It was very humid and the setting sun cast a dark eerie glow over the entire horizon. James felt different than usual. He felt stronger and more in control.

He looked down and saw that he was holding daggers in both his hands. Somehow, he knew that there was imminent danger as his senses went on high alert. Suddenly, James felt like he was torn in two parts, as if he was seeing himself through someone else's view. He knew that the person standing was him but it didn't feel like him. It felt more like a vision than it did like a dream now. He looked ahead and saw a woman standing, with his back turned towards him. She was wearing a mottled black leather pants and a simple white top with knee lengths boots. It wasn't how you'd usually dress, given the century but James realized that he was wearing something similar to that as well. The woman looked back at him and James breath caught in his throat, his 21st century self. His dream self-smiled and started chasing after her. It seemed like his dream self was almost waiting for this to happen. The 21st century James, however was ecstatic. He knew that she was the girl he had been chasing. As soon as he started going towards her she started running.

James yelled out at her to stop but she didn't turn back nor did she stop. He chased her through the forest, jumping on the fallen trees and dodging the hanging branches. The girl however, seemed to just go straight through them. Somehow that didn't faze the dream James at all. It was as if he expected this. James was much faster than the girl he was chasing and he soon got close enough to catch her. However, as soon as he would get close enough she would just slip away from his reach.

After chasing her for a long time he lost her in the woods. He immediately felt fear grip his chest. James knew that losing her was not supposed to happen. James had come a long way from where he stood before and even dream James was a bit confused. He had been relying on her to lead him through the forest but she had just disappeared. James looked around, everywhere trying to find her. He thought about the last place he had seen her before she had disappeared and the direction she was facing.

He decided that that would be the safest bet and he marked a tree with his dagger after which he ran as fast as he could, remembering the direction he came from. Deciding to follow the path where she was his ultimate destination was a good decision. He soon came to a clearing. In that clearing, he could see a very old castle. He could see that the girl was standing, back towards him, and he ran towards her. When he reached her, she did not notice that he was standing just behind her. She was just looking straight ahead at the castle with a weird expression on her face. He tried to see what she was looking at.

James looked straight ahead but it just looked like the ruins of an old castle. There was nothing fascinating about it, but the girl was looking intently at it. He looked at her, but she was no longer there. He looked around and she was standing behind him. He turned around and looked at her. There was something wrong with her face, though. It looked like it was rotten, like she had been buried under a mound of maggots for a couple of days. She opened her eyes and they were completely white, like somebody had sucked the life out of them.

Dream James smiled at that, while 21st century James completely lost his shit. He thought she was dead because she looked like a rotten corpse. Dream James, however, held both of his daggers at his sides and ran straight towards the girl. However, before dream James could reach her, she opened her mouth and let out a terrible scream and James was thrown off the ground. Just the sheer force of the scream was enough to make him fall on his back, at least ten feet away. The jerk was enough to wake James up, and he was completely covered in sweat again.

He felt cold and hot at the same time. He could still hear his ears ringing from the scream of the girl. He was sure that that was the girl he was after, but he could not figure out why she had lead him towards that castle or why she had screamed at him. His mind was working furiously on what he had dreamt about. It felt so real, as if he was actually present there. James was sure that that had actually happened, and that feeling of how he was given everything he needed to get to her, eased a bit.

He felt like he was getting closer to her. He still didn't know how that was possible, but he did. The weirdest part of the dream, or whatever the fuck that was, was how he felt now. Even though he was sweaty and grimy, he had a hard on. He didn't know why the fuck his heart thought that this moment would be the best to pump blood to his dick. But despite his efforts it still stayed erected and James felt ashamed of himself for not even being able to control his sexual desires.

He knew that it wasn't his fault for feeling the way he felt, however he felt ashamed that he felt aroused after what he had seen. *'You are fucked up.'* he said aloud to himself. Maybe it was being alone for so long, but James had taken to the habit of speaking to himself. He thought that if he didn't he would go completely dumb. He was looking outside his window when he was thinking about all of this and then he realized that something was not quite right. He concentrated outside and saw that he was not where he had slept. He was still sitting in his car but it was parked at the shore of a sea.

"How the fuck did I get here?" he thought. He knew that he couldn't have driven here all the way and yet again, he was forced to think that the supernatural was involved in this. *'Go with the fucking flow, I guess.'* James cursed and thought that everywhere he had ended up had been for a reason. Being here, at the sea, would also have a reason. He just had to find out what that was. He didn't know how being here would help him at all but he had to do something. It was late and the sun had gone down completely, and was now replaced by a crescent moon. He walked outside, barefoot into the sand. He had no idea what to do now, because he was pretty sure that he was

here for a reason. He had walked out and that was just about the end of his reasoning.

Why couldn't it be that he would be given a simple solution to all of this? He walked around looking for someone or something. He wasn't sure what he was looking for but he hoped that he would know once he found it. The beach looked beautiful and James looked like a retard walking alone on the beach. He had no idea what he was supposed to do so he just kept on walking, his eyes scanning everything that would indicate anything about finding her. He looked for anything weird or suspicious but the beach remained stoutly non-weird and unsuspicious. After wandering on the beach for quite some time, he had come a long way from where his car was parked.

He was standing near the water, however not close enough for the water to touch his feet. He turned around and saw at the end of the shore, a light. And then he felt very cold, on the particular spot he was standing at. It cold came out of nowhere. He looked around and saw nothing for miles except for the light he had seen far away from the shore. He walked forward and with each step he took he got warmer and warmer. It was as if the flame was beckoning him towards it. A small part of his mind tried to stop him but he didn't stop walking forward. He knew very well that it could have been a trap, but wasn't that exactly what he was trying to look for.

He kept walking forward and the flame burned invitingly, warming up the cold setting in James's chest. He finally got to the flame and saw a homeless woman standing beside a burning fire. He walked over there, mostly because he had nothing else to do. *"Hello,"* James said, *"mind if I join you?"* the old woman nodded yes and James stood by her side. She reeked of garbage and her face was smeared with dust and grime, like she had not bathed in a couple of years, which she probably hadn't. James wanted to get away from her, given how she smelled and how she looked. Under different circumstances, James would never have even given such a woman a second look, however his dreams had left him with an insatiable urge.

'Wow, you really wanna think about that now!?' James thought. His brain was being a dick right now. He decided to push the thought from his mind, and anyway there was no fucking way that he would do that with a homeless women. He wanted to leave right away, but the warmth from the fire and the exhaustion he felt after so many days he had not eaten was getting to him. His feet felt heavy, as if being sunk to the ground. A small part of his mind told him that he should get the fuck out of there, but James couldn't move his feet. His thought that his senses should be on high alert right now, given that he had woken up in a completely different place than he had slept in.

Maybe, because of the fact that he was in his car throughout, but he didn't feel alert at all. On the contrary he felt very drowsy, and suddenly the old woman didn't look so bad nor did she reek. He had been standing over there for a while and he was warm enough and wanted to leave. However, there was something that was holding him in his place. He could not even move a muscle. Suddenly the homeless women came closer to him and placed a hand on his face. And the smell returned.

Her fingers smelled like they were raked in piss and tar. He tried to move his face away from her but she had moved her hand to the back of his neck now. He felt disgusted by the fact that he felt aroused by that, but he did. It was an unnatural feeling, as if he was being forced into something that he did not want to do. Suddenly, she moved very close to him and before he knew it she had pinned him to the ground and even though James was very strong, somehow he was unable to get her off of himself.

Even though he had been weakened immensely he still should have been strong enough to throw that woman off, however, he couldn't even budge under her weight. Either he was much weaker than he thought he was, or she was much stronger than she looked. And James didn't feel that weak, so he was left with the only possibility that she was much stronger than she looked. The thought that she actually wanted to fuck him did not immediately cross his mind. He first thought that maybe it was just a mugging, and he was completely fine with that.

It wasn't until she started taking off her various jackets and scarfs that James thought, *'something sinister is going on here. I do not like this at all.'* She was completely naked on top of him. Her entire body was covered in wrinkles and hair and it was the most disgusting thing James ever had the displeasure to look on. He never thought that the sight of her naked woman would be what made him want to kill himself but there he was, lying on the sand, trying his best to touch as less of her as he could. He was nauseous and felt like vomiting. However, he could not even move.

He tried to stop her or push her off, or do anything to stop her but nothing seemed to be working, except his penis. James wanted to think that there was no way she could take his pants off, but he was mistaken. She pinned both of his arms with one hand and popped his belt buckle with the other. She wrestled his pants down and with her claw like hands and she tore open his shirt. James continually tried to get her off of himself but it was as if she had put him in some sort of a trance, so that he would have no choice but to submit to her.

That small part of his mind which was trying to stop him didn't seem so ridiculous now. He wished he had stopped and turned back however, now he was with a disgusting old woman who was riding him. James was already hard enough and weirdly enough he felt himself submitting to her. She grabbed his monster dong roughly. James winced hard at that he felt her shoving his one eyed monster in her and it was the weirdest feeling ever. He was hard as a rock but he could not bring himself even close to enjoying it. He felt sick to his stomach that this was happening to him, he kept trying to shout out, in hopes that somebody would listen and help him.

But for some reason his voice wouldn't work. He was left with no possible alternative except to finish what the old hag started. He had a sneaking suspicion that that was the only thing that would release him from her magic. As soon as he thought that, he was able to move. All thoughts of running away were gone from his mind because he knew that this was no longer a possibility. He shoved her aside and climbed on top of her. He still was not enjoying it even a bit, however he knew that he had to finish it.

He was on top now, and he kept on thrusting, wishing for the first time that he did not take so long to come. Finally, after what seemed like an eternity he came, letting out a slow moan and closing his eyes. *'You had no other choice.'* he told himself. He was already convinced that some supernatural shit was going on here and everything that was happening proved it. He knew that the only way this could have happened was if he was under some sort of spell.

He knew that all of this was being done to break his spirit, so that he would give up his pursuit and just give up on trying to find her. He wondered what he would tell her, when they finally met. He had done something so repulsive and appalling; he was sure that he would be rejected by her. The smallest part of him wanted to give up and just kill himself, but he could never do that. If he was being subjected to this, and he was just pursuing her. He wondered what fresh hell she was going through.

She must be in a lot of pain and suffering and the only way to stop that would be to go and find her. The uplifting thought of getting to her didn't do anything to make him feel good. He felt sick of himself. He couldn't believe that he had done this. Even though he was under a spell, he still couldn't stop blaming himself. He could have walked away when he had the chance, but he had walked straight towards the woman. He wondered if the entire reason he had woken up in this place was so that he could get fucking raped by a homeless woman.

He wanted to kill her, his mind felt completely in control now, however his body's strength wavered. He could feel himself trembling; he couldn't even stop his hands from shaking and felt like pathetic loser. *'One step at a time, Jamey boy. Come on!'* he whispered to himself. He marveled at how weak his voice had gotten. He didn't even sound like himself. His voice was usually very gruff and heavy now but he sounded like a little kid who just hit puberty.

His voice broke, mid-sentence, and he had to take a breath just to stabilize himself. He opened his eyes and looked around, but the woman was nowhere to be found. He realized that he was alone on the beach, completely covered in sweat and sand. He looked around to see where the homeless bitch had gone to. He looked straight ahead and straight ahead he saw a woman standing. Even though it was pitch black, with the only source of light being the flame beside which he had been raped, which was now extinguished, he could tell that it was a woman because he could see her long hair.

He tried to get up but he felt immensely weak. Like fucking the homeless woman had taken much more out of him than just physical exertion. He knew that it wasn't the fact that he had fucked the woman that made him weak. He had been with countless women and many more than one in one night and he never felt that way. He was sure that the woman was not human. The woman standing in front of him now, however, did not call him towards herself, nor did she show any indication that she had even noticed him.

He had seen enough shit for one night and was in no mood

to be fucked over again. However, one thing stopped him from crawling away. The small voice which had told him not to go to the homeless woman was now quiet. He didn't know if that meant that he was supposed to go to this woman, or if fucking the homeless woman had just made it so mad that it wasn't talking to him any longer. However, he thought that he might as well give this a chance.

He started crawling towards her. The entire beach was dark so he didn't know how he managed to see the woman's face, but he was sure that that wasn't the homeless woman. She wasn't even a woman, she was another species altogether, just like the homeless woman. James was sure of this because he had never seen normal women with blood red eyes. This wasn't the sort of eyes that you'd get if even if your eye had been internally ruptured, it was like her eyes were actually made of rubies but they weren't pretty at all. It gave her the look of a demon which was out to get him and only him.

She had paper thin skin under which all her veins were apparent; at least that's what James thought they were. It looked like tar flowing through her veins instead of blood and hair that fell in thick locks down to her shins. Looking at her, an immense fear gripped James. This was the first time that James had actually been afraid of something in his life. All he could do there was stand and ogle at this creature in front of him.

He had always thought of himself as the kind of guy who would manage to keep his calm no matter what the situation. However, looking at her, he wanted to run and hide. However, just as he was about to turn away, he stopped himself. *'I can face anything.'* And he did. He wasn't about to attack the woman, mostly because he couldn't even bring himself to stand up, but he wasn't about to run away either. She opened her mouth and from that a sound emitted, the same sound which James had heard in his dream. He was sent flying back and when he looked back up, the witch wasn't there and he was alone   on   the   beach.

Chapter 7
Lizard

James somehow managed to propel himself up and drag himself   back   to   his car. *"FUUUUUUUUUUUCCCCCCCCCCCCCCKKKKKKKKK KKKKKKKKKKK!"* He screamed at the top of his lungs. When he had arrived, there was nobody on the beach, though now there were several people over there. All of them looked at him like he was bat-shit crazy. He didn't give a fuck. He felt violated and disgusted with his own body.

He had just fucked a homeless woman who stunk worse than a dead body left in shit and piss for a week. He couldn't believe at what he had done to himself. He had stooped so low. He would rather have committed suicide, but somehow, at that time, but he couldn't push himself away from her. He had tried to get away from this woman. Unfortunately, his efforts were to no avail because she was strong. Very strong.

James never considered himself a weak man. In fact, he was very strong but somehow she was able to overpower him. If he were completely honest with himself, he wasn't even sure how the fuck it got to that point. He just remembered that he had woken up on the beach and then went there, because honestly, why the hell not. He remembered that he just saw the homeless woman and then they were fucking.

James pushed the thoughts out of his mind. He didn't want to think about something so horrid. He felt as if he were raped. At least that is what he thought. But at the same time, he felt disgusted. He could feel the stink rolling off of him. He reeked of the same smell that was coming from that woman. 'Fucking cunt!' he thought while gritting his teeth. He wanted to kill her for coming close to him, let alone touching him, but he couldn't remember seeing her on his way back to his car. But then, it suddenly hit him.

He had seen a woman standing on the beach after he had been fucked by the skunk. He was a hundred percent sure that it was the same girl he was looking for. But why had she screamed when he had seen her? He could still feel the goosebumps on his arms, and he was sweating and shivering. James's thoughts were scattered all over the place. He thought about the girl he had seen, about her face, he couldn't imagine it. Mostly because as soon as he had reached over there, she had screamed at him and after that, he couldn't remember anything.

Although he could still hear her scream in his ears; it was a wonder he hadn't lost his hearing. He had read somewhere that the scream of a banshee was terrible and was an omen of death.

He hadn't believed that at the time, but he felt that there was so much pain and sorrow in that scream it could only be an omen of death. He didn't want to think about what would happen next, especially if he thought that what he had heard was an omen of death. He didn't want to die, nor did he want her to die.

He hadn't gotten over her, nor could he ever get over her. The only thing that had sustained him until now was the thought that at the end of all this bullshit was finding her. He didn't even know her name, didn't know a single thing about her. But he did know that she belonged with him. He liked to take what was his no matter what the consequences were. He could deal with the consequences later. James got in the car, feeling weak and practically finished, he felt broken. He had just been raped and was nowhere closer to finding the one person he wanted more than anything in his life.

He didn't know what he was supposed to do, but then he remembered that he was supposed to rely on his instincts. Right now, his mind was just screaming that they needed a place to grab a shower. He marveled at the love he felt for her. Even though he was completely exhausted and broken, he only wanted a shower and then he would be back on the road. He could not stay put, nor did he want to. He knew that he would be sufficiently refreshed if he just took a shower and had something to eat.

He couldn't even remember when he last ate. He tried to pull out his phone but then realized that he was completely naked and was holding his cock. How the fuck could he not realize that? He was so disoriented that he had completely forgotten that after being fucked by the homeless woman, he couldn't find his clothes. He didn't care about anything that had gone with the clothes; his car was already unlocked and the keys were in the ignition and he had left his phone in the car as well. He couldn't thank the gods enough that he had done so, otherwise he would probably end up in jail and would have to call Harry.

For some reason, he didn't want to do that. Even though Harry was his best friend, something told him that he had to go through this alone. That woman was hard to find and he couldn't help but feel that if he asked for help, something would go wrong. To be honest, even if he did ask for help, what would he say? He imagined how the conversation would go. *"Hey, Harry. I am searching for this woman."*

"Damn bro! How is she?"

"She is so fucking beautiful man you have no idea. I think I am in love."

"Fucking A! Where'd you guys meet?"

"She came by the bar once."

"So you guys already did the dirty?"

"Not really. She came, I saw her and then felt nauseous, so I left."

"She didn't come back?"

"I haven't been to the bar since then."

"So why aren't you going back to the bar, maybe she'll swing back."

"Remember that time when I called you, almost crashed my car?"

"Yeah?"

"Yeah... umm that was because I saw her sitting in the back seat looking like a ghoul and she said, turn around."

"She said what now?"

"You heard me."

"So the girl was sitting in your car?"

"Not really. I just saw her for a moment and then I almost crashed my car."

"Ohkay? So... do you know her name?"

"Nope."

"Know where she live?"

"Nope."

"Do you know anything about her?"

"Nope."

"So how the fuck have you been trying to find her?"

"Driving around following my instincts. Would you help me?"

Yeah, that wouldn't exactly resonate sanely with Harry. That would be the most retarded conversation in the history of mankind and the more fucked up part would be, that Harry would actually help him try to find her. Like Harry was that good of a friend. He would just up and leave everything that he had going on just so that he could help James find her. James was sitting in his car and thought about what he should do next. He got his phone out and searched for the nearest hotel, guesthouse, AirBnB, motel, any place that he could get a hot shower. He found one called the Lizard that was just a five minute drive away. He started his car and started driving his car over there.

Even as he was driving, he tried to recall what exactly had happened when he had arrived at the beach. He tried to retrace his steps in his mind. He had woken up and was already at the beach, after which he had walked towards the beach. There was nobody on the entire beach and he was alone. He had only seen the homeless woman standing next to the fire, and he had been a bit cold so he went to stand next to her. Then the next thing he knew, they were having sex. She was very strong and he wanted to get away from her but he could not manage to move a muscle.

After they were done he looked around to see the homeless woman, but she was nowhere to be found. He looked around, remembering seeing the woman. Now that he was completely concentrated on thinking about what had happened, he found it very easy to recall. Seeing the woman, he was sure that it was the woman he was trying to find. Seeing her had given him a surge of energy. If not for her, he would have laid there and died. He was exhausted and broken at that moment, more so than he was now. He had crawled to her and then he had seen her, but he could not remember her face.

He looked in his rearview mirror and he had the most fucked up feeling. His mind went into overdrive and he saw the same woman he had seen on the beach sitting in his backseat, but it was different than the last time that had happened. He was not scared, because he knew that this was a figment of his imagination, that it was just his mind trying to connect two completely unrelated things so it could open a door. He saw her and then she disappeared. He could now remember her face.

Paper thin skin, blood red eyes and veins that looked like it was carrying tar instead of blood. She was very pale and it looked like she was malnourished, but he was sure that it was the same woman that he was chasing. However, the question remained, why the fuck did she scream? Even though the woman he had seen didn't look like a human at all, he was sure it was the same woman. She had the same face and the same hair, but somehow she was in this condition. He thought about what it could mean. He could come to the only conclusion that she would not survive much longer.

The way she looked was terrible. James knew that he would have to speed up doing whatever he was doing. If he were to describe it to anyone else, he would have said that he was just driving around aimlessly in the hopes that he could somehow run into her or find her. But he knew that what he was doing was not aimless. He was sure that wherever he was, whatever he was doing, he was on the right path. That he was actually closer to finding her. Somehow he had related the weird coincidences into him being closer to finding her.

He thought that this was happening just because he was too close to finding her. He knew that if he were to tell this to anyone, they would say that he had gone crazy. However, he knew that he was right. How else could he explain all the things that were happening? Especially since they were just so fucking unbelievable. Right now, he didn't care what anyone else thought. All he wanted was to go to the Lizard so he could take a shower.

On his way over to the Lizard, he saw a shop that was still open and he pulled over. He was about to get out but then he remembered that he was completely nude. So he looked around trying to see someone who could go in for him to buy him clothes. He saw a homeless man sitting beside the store and honked his car horn to get his attention. The homeless man looked up and came over to his window. As soon as he saw James, he started to go away but James rolled down his window. *"I swear I am not a weirdo. Just listen to me. I need clothes,"* he yelled out. He knew that the homeless man thought that something was very wrong and probably wanted nothing to do with that. However, when he said that he needed clothes, the homeless man stopped and turned around.

"I don't have any clothes," he said shortly. I know you dumb jackass, James thought. He didn't say it out loud though. *"I know friend. I'll give you a hundred bucks if you can go in there,"* he said, pointing to the store, *"and get me a pair of sweats and two shirts."* He pulled out the money and handed it to the man, *"You can have the rest."* *"You're weird,"* the

homeless man said as he gave James a disgusted look. Nonetheless, the homeless man took the money to get him his clothes. James waited for about five minutes before the homeless man returned and handed him his things. *"That cost forty bucks. You can have your hundred back if you want. I'll keep the sixty though,"* he said, handing the hundred back to James.

He looked at the homeless man and just said, *"It's alright. Keep it. Get yourself a room for the night and a hot meal."* Then, he rolled up the window and wore the sweats and shirt and drove the rest of the way to the Lizard. As soon as he got out of the car, he felt like he had been hit. He didn't feel pain or anything like that, he just felt as if he was about to lose his consciousness. He looked around and saw the same woman he had seen in his rearview mirror the first time. She was standing there and was mouthing something. He could not make out what she was trying to tell him.

So he went closer and as soon as he was close enough to hear her, he felt as if something pulled him back. James hit the ground and when he looked back up, the woman was gone. It was the ghoul who had appeared in his rearview mirror when he had almost crashed his car. He knew now that he was closer to finding her more than ever. He had thought that he would just grab a shower and then just leave. Now that this had happened, he knew he would have to see what was so special here that he had seen her here.

Chapter 8
Sibling Rivalry

He went inside the Lizard and it looked well-kept enough to have clean showers and clean rooms. *"Hello late comer!"* he looked around and saw the receptionist standing there. He was a weird looking man. The way he had greeted James, he knew that the man was strong. His voice was commanding and attention grabbing. He looked to be in his late forties, and his skin hung a bit loosely around his frame. However, James couldn't think of this man as weak. He was almost as tall as James and looked like he was power lifter back in his days.

James walked forward and shook the man's hand, so that he could confirm if he just looked strong or was actually strong. James grasped the man's hand hard and held on to it for a second with a firm grip. The man also grasped his hand hard and James intuition was right, the man had very strong. *"Would you like to book a room tonight?"* he asked. James looked at the man for a second before answering.

"Give me the best room you've got," he said. He knew that there was something peculiar about this place. He didn't know what it was but he could feel that it was somehow related to him searching for her. Somehow, all the feelings that he had

felt after the beach were gone. As if a door had been opened and James was on another level. He was actually able to feel his senses getting stronger and better.

"That's gonna run you…" he began but James cut him off.

"I don't care. Give me the best room you've got," he said. Hearing his own voice reverberating in his ears, James was a bit taken aback. He had always had a heavy and deep voice, but now he was commanding… like a dictator somehow. His accent sounded different too, in fact it sounded like an ancient dialect. His voice was even deeper now, heavier and with a hell of a lot more gravitas than he was used to.

"Sure, sir," the receptionist said. *"Under what name would you like to rent the place?"* he asked.

"James," he answered.

When the receptionist looked at him, he said, *"Just James."*

The receptionist nodded.

"Sure sir. I have put you in our elite suite," he said, handing the keys of the room to James. *"I am Carlton Frei, if you need anything you can call me and I'll be able to help you out."* James just nodded and took the keys. He was just about to go up to his room, but then he stopped. He had clothes but he would need more if he were to stay here for a bit.

"Can you get me some clothes? I suppose that would fall under anything, right?" he said, his voice low. For some reason he was having an out of body experience. He felt like he was on autopilot. He felt a familiar sensation, but at the same time he felt unfamiliar with himself. He decided that he would get to his room for now, and not dwell on that.

"That would fall under anything, of course. I can get you some clothes," Carlton said. Just as he had completed his sentence, James heard a bark. He turned around, and saw that a dog was standing just beside Carlton Frei and was staring intently at James.

"Oh this is my dog, Damascus. He was a stray when I found him, and since then he has been living with me. I tried to search for his owners but nobody showed up. So we are best friends now," he said. It was a Pitbull and it was huge. It stood almost to James's hip and it looked like it was a fighter dog. James felt as if he had been in this type of situation before as well. It was indeed a déjà vu. But then James shrugged that feeling off.

"Okay," he said. *"Send me the clothes as soon as you can, please,"* he added and went up to his room. He was still feeling the out of body experience. It was like he was doing everything but somebody else was controlling his mind. He

knew that it was not hostile but it felt ancient, like it had been alive for a thousand years and seen a lot of carnage. He was seeing images that he had never seen before, people that he had never seen before. He saw a castle and he saw people that he could not recognize but he knew that he was there. Everything that he was seeing looked so old, like it was from another century. He walked out of the elevator and into his room. He was pleased to see that the room was clean. He stripped and went into the bathroom to take a shower. He kept getting flashes of images, all of them moving too fast for him to comprehend. However, one image stuck out. It was him and a girl lying on a bed, but it was not like modern beds. It was the kind of beds they had in castles of old.

He tried to focus his mind's eye on the image and tried to see the girl's face, but he could not. She was resting her head on his chest and all he could see was the back of her head. He didn't know who it was. But given just how much had happened since he had come on this quest, he could not help but assume that it was the girl he was searching for. He got out of the shower and dried himself. He felt himself stronger than ever, as if a closed door had been opened.

He felt his senses were very sharply, and he could feel the position of everything in the room. He could feel now that everything was coming back into place. Like he had been on the correct path all along, but didn't know it. The decision to trust his instincts was very good, and now he knew why. His childhood, his boyhood, everything came back to him flooding back into his memory. He remembered the huge castle he used to live at. He remembered his own room, where he saw his bed. It was the same bed that he had seen in that image, lying with a girl.

He remembered everything. He was old, ancient. He had actually lost count of his age. He remembered waiting in the garden for Harry… seeing that woman and talking to her. He remembered what she said now. He had asked her what she wanted… and then his memory used to go completely blank. But now he remembered what she said.

"The gods and the fates are cruel. I have come here to warn you," she said.

"That doesn't make sense," he had replied.

"It will. You have been given an endless task. You have been destined for it because you put yourself in the middle of a feud as old as age itself. You still have the chance to make yourself free, but you're going to have to abandon the one you love most, the one you'd do anything for, no matter what the cost," she said.

"I don't love anyone that much," he said.

Under any and all circumstances, he would have thought that the woman was crazy, but he believed her.

"You will. When the time comes, you will have to make a choice. You will have to decide between yourself and between her. If you make that choice once, you will be bound for all eternity. If you choose yourself, you will live a normal life and die peacefully."

She looked at him with those huge eyes of hers. *"If you choose her, you will be bound. You will have to keep saving her until you find a way to end the feud, by reconciliation or by death,"* she said.

"Who is that girl?" James asked.

"You will find that out one day," she replied.

"You said that I'd be putting myself in the middle of a feud. I would be doing that by loving her?" he asked.

Since he already knew that the woman was telling the truth, he had to get as much out of her as possible.

"By loving her, by caring for her, by not wanting to let any harm come to her; yes," she answered.

"Why is she in the middle of a feud?" he asked.

"It is the rivalry of two siblings. For power. She has been blessed," she said.

She was having a hard time putting her thoughts into words. *"Her soul, her body, has been blessed. She has eternal life, but not like yours, if you make the choice. She is the only one, in the world, in history, in future, they can use as a pawn in their pursuit of power."*

James couldn't understand a thing she had just said, at that time. But he could now. He remembered everything now.

James had been born into a very wealthy family, thousands of years ago. This was why whenever he remembered his childhood, he used to think about huge halls and a castle. He had met the strange woman, and he was sure that she was not human. She had told him everything then, and he still didn't know why she had done that, or who she actually was. A couple of years after the meeting with the strange woman, he had met a girl. Her name was Sarah Alexandris. She was different than all the other girls he had met in his life.

She was special. Not just because she was different, but she just had something around her that made James sure that there was no one in the world like her. Even though they had known each other for years, she never told him about her family, nor did he ever meet them. But one night, she came to his castle, into his room. She seemed really scared but she wouldn't say anything. However, after James pestered her about it, she told him everything.

"My family has been blessed. Me specifically. My mother told me this when I was about ten. My father, he is a very cruel man. My mother was special which was why he had a daughter, me, with her. He was given a prophecy long ago, that if he was able to find the purest woman and have a daughter with her, he would always be able to find a way into power. His sister, she is stronger than he is. She would never let have any power more than her.

They lived together but he wanted to rule and his sister would never let him... he tried to usurp the throne but she managed to beat him. Since then, they have been trying to usurp each other. He knew about the prophecy so he found the purest woman in the world, my mother and had a daughter with her. He had to wait until I was eighteen so that he could use me to gain power. He has to sacrifice me... the power of my blood would give him enough power to usurp his sister. Both of them are after me. His sister is after me because she needs to kill me so that he won't be able to. He is after me because he needs to sacrifice me so that he can usurp his sister," she explained.

Then after pause, she continued, *"My mother is very learned in the magical arts, so she found a way to manipulate the prophecy. Prophecies are going to be fulfilled once they are made, so was this prophecy. But she managed to find a way to do both, satisfy the prophecy and give me a chance to live my life. If my father sacrifices me in between the ages of eighteen to twenty three, he would be able to usurp the throne. Otherwise he would have to wait for me to live my life."*

After learning all this, he remembered the woman's words. He had to make a choice. If he were to turn her away now, he would live a normal life. If he were to love her, to care for her, he would have be bound in destiny. He looked at her, deep in her eyes and kissed her hard. *"I am with you till the end,"* he said. After that time began an eternity long battle between James, Sarah's father and his sister. He was destined to save Sarah every time.

He also found out what the woman meant about Sarah's immortality being different from his. After he had told her that he was with her till the end, he had saved her from her father and his sister. They had lived a normal life, but James didn't age, not a single hair on his head turned white, but she did. She aged all the way up to forty-five, after which she died.

Even now, when James remembered her death the first time, he felt a pang of sorrow in his chest. He thought that everything was over, his life was over. He tried to kill himself, many times, but somehow he just never died.

One day as he went to Sarah's grave to grieve her passing, he met the same woman he had met all those years ago.

"I told you that the gods and the fates are cruel."

"I still would have chosen the same way I did. But why take her so soon? And why give me immortal life?"

"Why is everything that way it is? Why do you have two arms and not four? There isn't an answer to everything now, is there?"

"So now that she is gone, I am doomed to live out forever without ever meeting her again?" James asked.

He was afraid to hear the answer but he had to know it.

"That is not the case, no. You are alive for a reason. I told you that her immortality was going to be different than yours. While you live continuously, she has to die. A soul as precious and dangerous as her cannot be on the earth for too long. However the earth needs it too. So she will be reborn again. You will be here then as well. Your destinies are intertwined so you will meet again."

"I cannot wait for her to be reborn again. Help me please."

"What do you mean?"

"Make me forget that I ever met her. Please. I beg you."

"Things never leave the memory completely. They can only be closed behind a door, once that door opens, you will remember again. It will get worse every time until you find a

way to break the cycle completely."

"Do it. I'll find a way."

He had said that thousands of years ago, and he had not been able to find a way to break the cycle yet. After that, he had done the same thing over and over again. He could not find a way out. He wondered if this time would be different.

Chapter 9
The Last Act

James immediately felt pangs of guilt. He had chosen to forget everything that had happened, but the woman turned out to be right. He felt as if his heart had grown heavy and he was literally unable to move. He could not feel his arms or legs, nor could he think about anything other than Sarah. Every time she returned, she would have a different name, but somehow she would find him. He remembered every single one of those instances now.

Every time she had come into this world, every time she was born, she had chosen him, and all this while he had been clueless about her existence. Maybe she did that without knowing what she was really doing, but she did it nonetheless. This time around was no different, she was the one who came into the bar seeking him. He knew now that the old memories were knocking at his mind again, waiting to be unleashed.

He wasn't sure why it took him so long to remember it this time. When he had seen her for the second time, he remembered immediately about her. The next time it took a bit longer and a bit longer the time after that. He wasn't exactly sure what that meant, but he did have an idea about what it could mean. He was losing her slowly but surely. This time would be the last he would remember her.

At least, that was what he thought given how long it took him to remember everything about his past this time. He wasn't sure if the next time she came into his life, he would even be able to dredge up memories of her. It seemed like this was his last chance. James was a brave man; a warrior. He had fought for thousands of years, but the thought of losing her completely made him want to stop living. It made him want to go into a deep slumber from which he would never wake up. He tried to regain his composure, but the woman he had met at Sarah's grave was right. Every time he remembered it would be worse than the time before that. He laid down and tried to think about what he should do next.

****

Lumis knew she had won. The time was almost upon them for the girl to turn twenty-three and after that, Lumis would have won for good. This was the last time that James would be able to save her. She knew it for sure: even a soul as pure as her could be corrupted enough to be destroyed completely. This was it, her complete victory. She knew that right at this moment, her brother, Damascus, would be planning to manipulate the foolish James in such a way that it would free

Lucy from her grasp. He was always like that, she thought. Didn't he know that he could never usurp Lumis, no matter how much he tried?

He still hadn't grasped just how manipulative she was, and how easy it was for her to take advantage of everyone and everything she needed. All she had to do was ensure that he could not get at Lucy until she became useless, which was at the age of twenty-three. She was the one who gave Lucy's mother the idea to manipulate the prophecy. Now all she had to do was to stop her brother from coming into power otherwise he would wreck it all up. The power afforded to her and her brother by the gods was given to them because they had helped the gods stay in power. In return, the gods wanted to repay them. So after discussing it among them, the siblings asked for their own kingdom, where they could live and have power.

They wanted so much power that, no matter whoever attached their land, would never be able to defeat these two siblings. The gods had granted their wish and given them a piece of land, where they would be able to do anything. For the longest time, they had the power and ruled over their own kingdom, but then her brother got greedy and wanted the throne for himself. She had always known that he was power hungry, but she never thought that he would come after her. She had taught him everything he knew, and she was the reason that they had managed to successfully help the gods, and secure their own kingdom ruling rule over the people of their homeland.

Had it not been for her, they would have rotted away after their death. But she helped him navigate eternal life and end up with an entire kingdom to rule over for all eternity. None of it mattered to Damascus. But like the Queen she was, she stayed one step ahead of him, banishing him from the kingdom when he tried to realize his ambitions. He had never been powerful enough to take her on, nor was he intelligent enough to rule over his own life, let alone a kingdom. He wanted to expand their kingdom and he wanted more, even though he didn't know what to do with it if he'd achieved it.

However, she knew very well that she had bargained with the gods to give them a kingdom and they had given her what they believed should be enough for them. Conquering other lands could have angered the gods as siblings would have effectively broken their word with the gods. She knew about the gods, they never liked mortals, nor were they happy about Lumis and Damascus helping them out. But they had to pay their debts. They would be looking for a reason to take that away. She could not let that happen.

She had told that to Damascus countless times but he was blind to it. He held firm on the belief that since he was immortal, he could not be harmed. He failed to understand that even though they could not be harmed, they could be caged or silenced forever into complete obscurity. Once he got the idea to seize her throne, she knew that he would never rest until he had succeeded. She had been able to stop his attacks every time, until the last time. He had managed to get dangerously close to actually sacrificing Lucy, and actually overthrowing her.

She cursed the gods, they were the ones who had woven faith in such a way that he would always have a way to overthrow her. They had promised her a kingdom and they had granted her promise at the time. She thought that that was it, but she should have known that they would never give her anything for all eternity. Lumis was a just leader and she had ruled over her people with love and peace. Together, they had progressed and they had invented. They were the ones who were able to make humanity come out of the dark ages and into the age of light and peace. The gods couldn't bear the thought that they were able to do that without their help.

So in order to destroy them, they had first taken away her kingdom by giving her brother an eternally unsatisfied thirst to overthrow her. His constant attacks on her kingdom had destroyed the civilization she worked so hard to create. Slowly yet surely, she began to figure it all out. Although the desire to rule and outshine his sister had always been present in Damascus, but he had been able to suppress it for some time. He wouldn't have attacked her again and again unless it was for the gods. They were the ones who had driven him insane. She had to tip her hat at the gods, nonetheless.

She had always loved a good strategy and the one they had employed to run her out of power was one of the best that she had seen. By turning her brother against her, they had ensured that she would not be able to rule her kingdom, and if Damascus was able to overthrow her he would try to conquer other lands. Then they would be able to break their promise and cage them for all eternity. Either way, they would win. She was sure that there must be some way to ensure that her brother would never be able to even try to attack her again. So she started on her quest, to try to find everything she could about the forbidden arts. She was sure that the answer lay in it, and she was right. She hunted for thousands of years, all the while constantly fighting and defeating her brother. Finally, she was able to locate the books, the oldest books that taught her a great deal. When Damascus first attacked her, in hopes of taking power by force, she had managed to defeat him, but she wanted to take the safer path for the next time.

Mostly, because she wanted to defeat the gods now, if they believed that they would be able to take back their promise and outsmart her, they should have had another thought coming. She would cage her brother, making him incapable of ever attacking her again, and then she would rule her kingdom again, in peace and forever. Her brother's attacks had been getting more lethal, he had been studying her and trying to attack her in different ways. She knew that she was stronger than her brother, but still wanted to be absolutely sure that he would never be able to overthrow her.

So she hunted the books written by the oldest civilization containing knowledge given to them by the gods themselves. Using that knowledge, she had turned her brother into a dog, and condemned him into being that way for eternity. But even that had been unable to hinder his insatiable thirst for power. Before she turned him into a dog, he had been able to impregnate the purest woman in the world, who gave birth to Lucy. Even now he was trying to overthrow her using his own daughter.

In a fit of rage, she had taken Lucy's mother and imprisoned her, slipping her into a trance, which would infinitely slow down her ageing so that she would never die. As a result, he would never be able to impregnate her nor would he ever be able to father a daughter. However, the girl had proven resilient every time she had dealt with her. This time she had been able to escape her clutches faster than she had been able to before.

That had annoyed her so much that she had vowed to kill her once she had turned twenty-three. She didn't know what would happen if she killed her before she turned twenty-three, though she did know that she didn't want to face the consequences.

But, she wouldn't have to wait long. The girl was turning twenty three in a day and she would then be free forever. She finally had all the pieces of the puzzle within her grasp. She had Lucy's mother, and she had Lucy, she had transformed her brother into a dog and she was going to kill the girl. She had found out that the girl's soul was special and of the earth. Her essence was tied to the earth, so all she had to do was ensure that she never return to the earth. Killing her and capturing her essence, her soul and her body was the only way to guarantee that.

Just one more day and then she would have everything she wanted; she would have defeated her brother, and James, as well as the gods who wanted regained her kingdom. She knew that the bigger threat among them was James. However, she had her bases covered. She had found out his greatest weakness. It was the same as all men; sex. She had tempted him with sex until now. She manipulated him into having sex with a homeless woman and made him lose his mind over her when he first saw her. She knew that no matter what happened, he would never be able to resist the temptation that she would encapsulate him with. He was never able to nor would he ever be able to stop himself.

****

James woke up with a single thought in his mind, no matter what happened he would have to save Sarah today. He liked to remember her by her original name, it felt better for him somehow it felt like he had a deeper connection with her. He remembered the place he had gone to rescue her the last time, and knew that he had to go their again. He remembered the witch who had possessed Sarah, Lumis Ash. In all his years, he had never been able to understand the actual story, each time he had been way too pre-occupied with saving Sarah. He had never bothered to think about why all this was happening.

Maybe that's where he would find the answer. He would have to somehow find out the reason why all this was happening. He got out of bed and knew the where he had to go. He remembered very well where the witch lived and he knew that if he were to ever save her, that's the place he needed to be. He got out of bed, went to the lobby and checked out. He got in his car and drove like a crazy man all the way to Lumis's castle. It was barely dawn now and somehow, he instinctively knew that today would be his last chance to save her, he would never be able to do it after this day.

148

Finally after driving for about an hour, he reached the castle. But as he came within two hundred yards of the castle, he somehow crashed, badly. He felt as if his car had hit a concrete wall. He lost control of the wheel and his car completely turned over, rolling off the road and throwing him out. He didn't care about any of that though. He was immortal and he knew that he couldn't get hurt. The SUV was the least of his worries at the moment. But he knew that this accident was not a coincidence. His G-Wagon was in peak condition and he knew that there was no way that it could malfunction.

This had to be the work of the witch. He got up and looked around to see what he had hit, and just as soon as that though came, he was thrown off his feet. He tried to see what was throwing him around but his eyes were full of sand. Suddenly, he got the weirdest feeling, as if he was becoming hard. He didn't know how that was happening but he just knew that he felt a tingling sensation in his pants. He got up and rubbed his eyes, he looked up and saw a pig staring down at him.

The rational part of his brain knew that there was no way in hell there could be a pig in these parts but the carnal part of him found that pig to be the sexiest thing alive. The way he was feeling right now, he would fuck the dirt if it were up to him. He walked forward, every step he took he wanted to turn towards the castle and go there, but he just could not help himself.

******

Fool! Lumis thought. Thousands of years of life and another thousand years guaranteed couldn't teach a man the self-control needed to master their desires. She had felt him coming a long way off. She knew that Lucy was only able to regain control or become stronger if she felt any emotion; be that anger, happiness or sadness or if James was particularly close to her. She had felt her getting stronger when she was near the Lizard. At that time, she tried to use that to her advantage. She couldn't let him stay in the Lizard, where Damascus could try to manipulate him, but he had gone right in there.

She knew that now, James was here because she could feel her getting stronger again. She knew just how to manipulate him into staying away. She would have let him have her, but she needed Lucy to stay with her, because she needed her essence to ensure that she could once again rule over her kingdom. If her life was what was needed to pursue the advancement of humanity without the interruption of gods, then she would have to die. She was doing it all for the greater good.

She had known about the gods interfering in the matters of humanity since the dawn of man, hindering them and slowing down their progress at every nook and turn. She would be the one to save humanity, no matter what the cost, and here the cost was just the life of a single girl and the will to live of her lover. If that was the cost, she would gladly trade it; they were expendable... she wasn't. She had to live on. She had sent one of her minions, the same woman she had sent to hinder him when he was at the beach.

She was sure that he wouldn't be able to resist her, and she needed to break him. She was just done with this shit. She would destroy him if need be, because she knew that even after she had defeated her brother, she would still have to deal with him, even if she killed Lucy. He would still try to take revenge, and since he was immortal, that was just another hassle that she did not want to get into. She would enslave him. Fucker thought that he was destined for a happy ending, when all he did was think with his dick.

She would see his destruction with her own eyes. She was still possessing Lucy's body, which was the only way to make sure that she would not escape, she walked out of her castle and looked at the abysmal actions taking place. There was no way he would ever be sane again, not that he was ever sane. Who would ever choose a life like this? She looked at him and saw him pinned down by the pig she had sent after him and then she saw nothing.

****

Some part of James knew that Sarah needed him, yet here he was trapped under a pig… the worst part was that he was enjoying himself immensely. He wanted to throw the pig off of himself, he was conscious and knew what was happening. However, he also knew that he would never be able to. He put his hands around the belly of the pig, flipping it over and getting on top. As he was doing this he looked up and saw her. Both of them called out to each other and he felt his urge subside enough to go to her.

TURN AROUND

www.ingramcontent.com/pod-product-compliance
Lightning Source LLC
Chambersburg PA
CBHW051141020726
47501CB00005B/1617